# THE GOOD BADMAN

Three tales of the Old West. When Speedy overhears a conversation between the outlaw Lynch brothers, planning a kidnapping and murder, he's determined to stop the crime before it occurs. The would-be killer is well-mounted, while Speedy has only a mule — but he may be able to succeed by outwitting him . . . A Yankee sharpshooter climbs into a tree above a Confederate trench and begins picking off the soldiers one by one: taking his time, and spotting the best men to kill. There must be a way to stop him . . . Ed Garver was known in his prize-fighting days as Kid Denver. Now his career in the ring is behind him, and he is back in the West on his old range. Les Burns, his one-time adversary, is now a successful attorney — and has a job for him . . .

# THE GOOD BADMAN

## A WESTERN TRIO

## MAX BRAND®

SAGEBRUSH
Large Print Westerns

First published in the United States by Five Star

First Isis Edition
published 2017
by arrangement with
Golden West Literary Agency

A catalogue record for this book is available
from the British Library.

ISBN 978–1–78541–385–8 (pb)

# Contents

# SPEEDY'S DESERT DANCE

Frederick Faust's saga of the hero Speedy began with "Tramp Magic", a six-part serial in *Western Story Magazine*, which appeared in the issues dated November 21, 1931 through December 26, 1932. As most of Faust's continuing characters, Speedy is a loner, little more than a youngster, able to outwit and outmaneuver even the deadliest of men without the use of a gun. He appeared in a total of nine short stories in addition to the serial. The serial has been reprinted by Leisure Books under the title *Speedy*. The first short novel, "Speedy – Deputy", can be found in *Jokers Extra Wild* (Five Star Westerns, 2002); "Seven-Day Lawman" can be found in *Flaming Fortune* (Five Star Westerns, 2003); "Speedy's Mare" appears in *Peter Blue* (Five Star Westerns, 2003); "The Crystal Game" is in *The Crystal Game* (Five Star Westerns, 2005); "Red Rock's Secret" in *Red Rock's Secret* (Five Star Westerns, 2006); "Speedy's Bargain" in *Treasure Well* (Five Star Westerns, 2006), "The Nighthawk Trail" in *Rifle Pass* (Five Star Westerns, 2007), "Outlaws from Afar" in *Outlaws from Afar* (Five Star Westerns, 2007). "Speedy's Desert Dance", the last of the nine short stories, first appeared in the January 28, 1933 issue of Street & Smith's *Western Story Magazine*.

# CHAPTER
## ONE

In the dappling of shadow under a cottonwood, Speedy lay, the very picture of that laziness and ease that had caused certain foolish men, long ago, to give him his nickname. All the lines of his slender body flowed as smoothly, with as soft an inertness as the lines of a panther stretched on jungle grass. Only the eyes of the panther will stay alert. And the eyes of Speedy were alert, also. He seemed to be almost unconscious, and yet hardly a leaf could stir on the tree above him without his knowledge.

He wore the clothes of a Mexican laborer — white cotton trousers so frayed at the bottom that they were rolled up to his brown knees, a shirt open at the throat, a rag of a sash about his waist, and straw-soled *huarachos* on his feet. The meagerness of his clothes let his body be seen more closely. To a careless eye, he seemed too light, too frail; it needed an artist to appreciate the exquisite nicety with which that mechanism was fitted together, the roundness, the smooth-flowing interplay.

The straw hat was under his head, and the wind ruffled in the black of his hair, sometimes moving it like a shadow on his forehead. He looked like a Mexican;

3

there was a Latin delicacy and beauty of feature. And when he half smiled at a thought, his smile was the white Latin flash in a brown face.

He was aware of the coming of the two men, long before their shadows crossed him. From the corners of his half-closed eyes he was aware of them for what they were, twin brothers in bulky size, in brutal good looks. He was aware of the slight flaring of their nostrils, the stiffness about their mouths. Nature had given them some of these animal characteristics; whiskey had accentuated them. In the young eyes of Speedy there was the wisdom of old age; he noted above all the big hands of these men, and the guns that were strapped low down on their thighs. The left arm of one was slung in a bandage.

"We can talk private here in the shade, Steve," one of them was saying.

"There's somebody here already, Tim," said the other.

"There ain't anybody. There's only a greaser," said Tim.

"Sure, it's only a greaser." Steve chuckled. "Up, bum, and start movin'!"

The eyes of Speedy opened a little more, only a little. They were as bright and as coldly dangerous as ever the eye of a panther could be, before it leaps.

"He don't hear you," said Tim.

"I'll open his ears," said Steve, who wore the bandage. "Up!" He ground the toe of his boot into the ribs of Speedy.

Speedy sat up. "No spik English, señor," he said.

"You no spik English? You get out, just the same," said Steve.

Speedy rose to his feet without touching the ground with his fingers, with a single easy movement of his body. He made no protest, and walked slowly off, his shuffling *huarachos* bringing up wisps of dust. He moved a little closer to the wall of the inn, and then slumped again to the ground, as a tired dog lies down, all in one move.

He had for shade, now, the shelter of a mesquite. But the mesquite foliage makes no more than a misting of the light, holding its little varnished leaves edgewise to the burning of the sun so that it will lose as little water as possible by evaporation. It was, therefore, almost in the full glare of the sun that Speedy lay down, with his straw hat again under his head. But the burn of that sun he could endure. He let the fierceness of it soak into his flesh, and smiled a little. He seemed sound asleep, in a moment, and, when a whirlpool of dust was raised by the wind and walked toward him, he did not stir as it crossed his face with its vortex.

"Look at him," said Steve, "rolling in the dust and soakin' up the sun. Can he hear us?"

"What difference? He don't understand," said Tim. "Now, blaze away."

"I got the cablegram today," said Steve. "I can't go. You can."

Speedy turned his head a little. Through the lashes of his eyes he studied the pair carefully. And his ears strained. Some of the words that followed, he could hear clearly enough; others were more than half lost;

others were mere murmurs that contained no syllables. What he made out was that the cablegram called for instant action; that Steve could not go on the mission; that Tim would have to ride.

"And when I get there?" said Tim.

Steve raised his right hand and crooked the trigger finger in suddenly. Tim shook his head in violent disagreement.

And Steve exclaimed something. Speedy's ears caught: ". . . Materro wants! That's all."

It was perfectly clear. Someone was to be shot. "Materro" wanted it done. And Tim was to do it.

Presently the two men walked down the street. Speedy went behind them as far as a cluster of men who were in front of the hotel, where they stood talking loudly, with many gestures. There the two paused to speak with friends, and Speedy brushed by Steve. In his hand he took away the cablegram form that had been in Steve's coat pocket. Turning into the next lane, he opened the paper and read:

*ISABELLA ESCAPED AND PROBABLY ON SAILING SHIP BOUND FOR SAN GALLO ARRIVING BETWEEN TENTH AND TWENTIETH STOP FINISH NOW*

*Materro*

Speedy folded the slip again. The grisly thing went like a finger of ice over his brain. Was it a woman who was to be murdered? No, she was not to arrive at San Gallo until between the 10th and the 20th. It was the

**6**

9<sup>th</sup>, that day. And Materro wanted something done at once. "Finish now." That was the word that brought death to someone.

He turned back from the corner in time to see Tim and Steve disappearing across the street through the swinging doors of a saloon. Speedy stopped to think. There was murder in the air, and every nerve of his body was set to prevent it. The boot that had kicked him in the ribs had not injured his body, but it had wounded his pride, and the pride of Speedy, in spite of his appearance, was like the pride of an eagle in the air.

If he were to prevent the killing, he must either keep Tim from leaving the town, or else he must follow the man and stop his hand at the vital moment. Follow him where? To San Gallo? Was that the name of the place where the murder was to take place?

Speedy went first to the stable behind the hotel and got out his mule. It was a good, tough gray, with the strength of iron in it, and it was almost ideally suited for carrying a rider patiently, steadily over the thirsty leagues of the desert, where the water licks were drying up. The dry marches that mule could make were prodigious things. But it lacked speed, of course, and speed was probably what Tim would use.

Speedy looked the mule over with a sigh of despair. It was not fast enough to head off Tim. And he had not enough money to change the brute for a good running horse. However, he knew how to make the best of a bad bargain.

With the mule saddled, and the narrow roll of his pack strapped behind the saddle, Speedy jogged down the street and stopped in front of the saloon into which the two brothers had disappeared.

He dismounted, opened a large canvas saddlebag, and took from it a guitar. He was tuning it as he entered the swinging doors.

After the hot desert air outside, the moist coolness of the place passed like the touch of water over his skin. But a big red-faced man with an enormous paunch shouted at him from behind the bar:

"Out, greaser! No greasers in this saloon!"

Speedy took off his straw hat and bowed. He commenced to back toward the door, still bowing, still smiling, but he backed very slowly.

"I, señor," said Speedy, "only sing and dance for the *Americanos*. I never raise my head to drink with them."

"Damn him and his singing," said the man with his arm in the sling. He was standing at a little distance down the bar, with a glass of red-brown whiskey shining in his hand. "Throw him out, Barney."

"Yeah, get out!" roared Barney, the bartender. "Get out and stay out, unless you can sing like a regular bird. You take your chance. Want to try it? Get out now, unless you're pretty sure you'll please us, because, if you don't, we'll kick you out, and, when you light, you'll bust most of your bones."

Speedy no longer retreated. He even stepped forward, and replaced the hat on his head.

"I am your servant, señor," he said, "and, being your servant, I should not fear to please you. Is Mexican music what you want?"

8

"Yeah, give us a greaser song," said Tim. "Tune it up and let's have it."

Instantly Speedy struck the resounding strings of the guitar, and then, plucking them rapidly, and not with too much strength, he started the accompaniment, and raised his voice.

*I'll give them a song and dance that will please them, now,* he thought to himself. *But across the desert, there'll be dancing in more ways than one. I'll lead some people a desert dance there, all right, before I get through.*

Tim and Steve instantly sidled between him and the door, to block his retreat. A glance at their faces showed that they were anxious for the song to end, not because they disliked the music but because they wanted the pleasure of beating the Mexican.

Speedy sang a song of the wine making, far south, of the purple dust on the grapes, of the juices that spurt out from beneath the treading feet of the wine pressers, of the fragrance of the new wine, of the nights pale and bright with stars, and the days white with a powerful sun.

He sang, and then, still keeping the accompaniment going, but making it suddenly loud, he started dancing. The straw *huarachos*, whispering and crinkling against the floor, flew almost faster than the eye could follow.

Steve and Tim, by the door, were eying the dance, as they had listened to the song, with sneering malice in their faces. But Barney, the bartender, leaned over the bar with a wide grin of pleasure, and presently began to beat time with the flat of his hand.

9

Finally Speedy stopped plucking at the guitar and devoted all of his attention to the dance alone, spinning and whirling here and there on his flying feet, his arms outstretched to keep the balance secure.

In the midst of that whirling, he drifted close to the two brothers near the door and, with an unseen gesture, passed the cablegram back into the pocket of Steve.

Speedy went on spinning in the dance, until it carried him behind the big couple and the swinging doors.

Instantly the powerful hand of Tim collared him and hurled him staggeringly back toward the center of the long, narrow room,

"You can't run out on us, you sneak!" shouted Tim.

"Let him alone, Tim Lynch!" shouted the bartender.

But Speedy, coming out of the stagger from which he had nearly fallen to the floor, was continuing the dance. Even his smiling had not stopped, and, as for the flash of his eyes, it might well be mistaken for the mere gleam of a singer's eyes, and not for the hate and rage that were burning in him like a fire.

# CHAPTER
# TWO

The dance ended with Speedy taking off his hat and making a wide and deep bow. He smiled on the bartender and he also smiled on the two handsome, brutal faces of Tim and Steve Lynch that leered at him.

The bartender beat more loudly than ever on the bar.

"That's the best song and dance that I ever seen," he declared.

"Wait a minute," said Tim Lynch, still smiling, while his eyes surveyed the slender body of Speedy. "Wait a minute, will you? There's gotta be a vote on this here. You vote that it's a good song and dance, but, if you're voted down, that greaser gets kicked out onto the street. How you vote, Steve?"

"Rotten!" said Steve, fairly shouting. "There wasn't no music to the song, and there wasn't no sense to it, neither. And the dancing was kind of out of step, seemed to me. Rotten, I'd say."

"That's what I say," remarked Tim Lynch. "There ain't any more music in that gent's throat than there is in my feet. Out he goes."

He made a sudden reach for Speedy.

He missed his hold, as though he had reached for a dead leaf, so lightly, so easily did Speedy avoid that hand. But he had made one mistake. He had looked upon the man with the bandaged arm as a negligible property in the brawl, but now big Steve Lynch, his step lightened by malice, his eyes squinting, came swiftly in. He did not try to catch Speedy with his hand, but used his fist.

At the last instant, Speedy saw the flying danger come near. He could not avoid it entirely, and, as he swerved, the heavy knuckles of Steve glanced along the side of his head. The weight of the blow flung Speedy back against the wall, his head and shoulders striking heavily.

Helpless as he was for the instant, serious damage might have come to him. But now Barney charged in between. He had taken this time to get around the end of the bar, and now he stood between Speedy and danger.

"You fellows can run the place down there at San Gallo," said Barney, "but you ain't runnin' my saloon. Not half! Leave him be. He ain't your size, and you've scared the poor kid to death and broke his head for him."

In fact, the eyes of Speedy were a little distended and rolling. It might have been purest rage that worked in him, but the bartender chose to take it for fear.

Steve Lynch, in spite of the fact that one arm was bandaged, seemed eager to step in past Barney and get at the victim, but Tim restrained him.

"Take it easy, Steve," he said. "We've give the greaser something to think about. He ain't goin' to be so sure about his song and dance from this time on. He's goin' to be scared, when he gets out among folks, and that's the way that a greaser had oughta be. Come back there to the end of the room. I wanna talk to you some more, before I start."

He turned to Barney.

"Give us a couple of whiskies," he said.

The whiskies were forthcoming, and the pair of big brothers retired to the end of the room, while Barney, clapping Speedy on the shoulder, said: "Don't take it too hard, young feller. We got some rough gents in this part of the world, and the Lynch boys is among the roughest. Stand up and have a drink with me, and forget that clip you got alongside the head. Lucky it didn't land square, or there would've been a busted head for you, and no mistake."

Speedy stood at the bar, trembling. In all his life, anger had never come so near to mastering him, but anger now was the last thing that he dared to show. What was important was that he should learn all he could of the plans of the Lynch brothers and discover, if possible, the identity of the person they were to kill.

So he stood at the bar, facing a little toward the other pair, and studying their faces through the shadow. Tim Lynch was lost to him, for the head of Tim was turned away from him. Of the voices he could understand no more than an occasional exclamation, and hear a steady muttering. But there was a pale shaft of light falling from a window upon the face of Steve, and that light enabled him, now and then, to read the lips of Steve for a few instants. Speedy saw him say:

"Crocker's gotta die . . . that's all. He's gotta die, and you've gotta kill him."

It seemed from the shaken head of Tim that he dissented to this, and Steve leaned forward, his face partially hidden behind his hand, to argue the point.

The argument did not need to last long; Tim was readily convinced, according to the manner in which he soon was nodding his head.

Then Steve was saying: "The boys are all solid, now, except that old fool of a Danny. And you can brush him out of the way. Then get Lew Crocker and get him good. I wish I was goin' to be there . . ."

Again his hand partially covered his lips, and Speedy, burning with curiosity, quivering with eagerness, could make out no more of the words that immediately followed.

But he had learned a great deal.

At San Gallo, wherever that might be, Tim Lynch would find that "the boys were now all solid," and that it would be easy to kill a man named Lew Crocker, because Crocker's only friend was an old chap named Danny.

Why not call in the sheriff for this occasion? Surely the law was needed.

But Speedy, thinking the matter over as he sipped his drink at the bar, decided that he would never be able to interest the powers of the law. All that he had discovered was hardly more than hearsay. As a matter of fact, he had not even heard, but merely seen some of the words on the lips of Steve. He would be laughed at. These fellows were known. They were familiar figures. He was a stranger and, to all appearances, no more than a poor greaser. The sheriff would probably throw him out of his office, if he tried to tell his tale. Yes, or put him in jail as a mischief-maker and hobo.

Speedy thanked the bartender and went out into the street. There, in the burning strength of the sunshine, he touched the swelling on the side of his head where the iron-hard knuckles of Steve had glanced.

What had happened to him today had never happened before in all his life. To the blunt and heavier strength of other men he had always been able to oppose a rapier deftness of hand and wit that turned blows and dangers aside. Now he had been bruised, humiliated, kicked about like a dog.

Somewhere there would he a counter-reckoning. The day might come when Lew Crocker, whoever he was, would have another friend than Danny, in the time of need.

A Mexican peddler of a mule load of odds and ends came down the street, and Speedy turned in at his side. This was a fat fellow with a rosy face, and a wandering eye that searched all who came near, in his hunt for a customer.

"Where shall a poor man find a chance to work?" asked Speedy. "I hear of a town called San Gallo."

"That's no town," said the peddler. "That is no place at all for our countrymen. It is a ranch where nothing but the *gringos* work."

"I heard of it," said Speedy sadly.

"Forty miles south, toward the sea," said the other. "I know it. I know all of this country better than a hawk knows it. A green lagoon is stuck into the side of the land, and at the end of the lagoon there is a ranch house. That is all. That is San Gallo. No town, but a ranch."

"And no Mexicans work there?" asked Speedy.

"Not one," said the other. "The *gringos* only . . ."

There was a heavy beating of hoofs.

"Out of the way, greasers!" shouted a heavy voice.

And between them galloped Tim Lynch on a big black horse. The dust, cupped and flung upward by the hollow hoofs of the horse, hung in a blinding cloud, and through it Speedy dimly saw the man disappear, with the red of his bandanna fluttering rapidly behind his neck.

Speedy was on the back of his mule at once.

To follow that rider was almost like trying to keep the trail of a flying comet, but he would attempt the task.

He felt that already he had failed in almost every point. For one thing, he had wanted to keep Tim Lynch from leaving the town. For another, he had wanted to learn more particulars of the place that was now his goal. But all he knew was that San Gallo was a ranch many miles to the south, where a green lagoon thrust into the land from the Gulf of Mexico.

On that place he might find Lew Crocker, whose life was endangered. There was a woman, Isabella, who seemed to be connected with the story at some point. There was also Materro, a sinister influence in the background who could tell the Lynch brothers when to act.

The whole matter was a mystery, and Speedy had only the speed of a gray mule to use on the desert trail.

# CHAPTER
# THREE

It was a time to make haste slowly, Speedy knew. He simply kept the mule to a steady dog-trot, with the dissolving dust cloud made by Tim Lynch vanishing before him.

Behind him, the little town dwindled, drew together to a line of blinking windows, and then gathered to a point that disappeared behind the first low swale of ground.

Before him lay open desert country, gray country, with dusty, sun-dried grasses glowing in obscure patches, here and there, although now and again he saw a scattering of cattle grazing.

Twice he almost lost the trail of Tim Lynch, but he managed to spot it again, where the man had turned both times to the left onto smaller trails. He knew the track, by this time, and the barred shoe on the left forehoof. His confidence increased, and he kept the mule steadily to that trot.

The dust cloud that Lynch made with his black had disappeared, and it did not grow up again as the miles drifted behind Speedy. Then he saw the trail leading down toward the pale gray-green willows of a watercourse.

He dismounted on the verge of them and went on foot. The pungency of tobacco reached him first. Then, on the bank of a semi-stagnant pool, he saw Tim Lynch stretched on his back with his hands under his head. The black grazed a patch of grass twenty steps away. The big horse was rather badly spent, and no doubt the pause had been made by Lynch to rest it at a halfway point down the trail.

The obvious thing was to take the horse and let the man proceed on foot. Cowpunchers are notoriously helpless when they have to walk. And certainly it should not take long after the arrival of Speedy at San Gallo to warn Lew Crocker of the danger that was now approaching him.

Yet it was a savage temptation to put hands on Tim Lynch here and now. Speedy fought that temptation back. Instead, he turned himself into a snake-like body that worked softly through the underbrush until it came near the black horse.

The cinches had been loosened. Speedy rose like a shadow, drew the cinches taut, and, without stopping to tie them, whipped into the saddle. Behind him, he heard a shout, then a wild yell of rage. A gun barked. A bullet beat into a tree trunk nearby. But Speedy already was flying the horse among the willows, back toward the point where he had left the gray mule.

He dismounted there, tied the cinches of the black horse, took the gray mule on the lead, and rode on again. He was far off on the head of a low hill when, looking back, he saw the big form of Tim Lynch issue from the trees and run in frantic pursuit, throwing up dust almost like a galloping horse.

Speedy laughed, as his eye for an instant caressed that laboring form. Much of the forty miles remained. It would be a very weary Tim Lynch that finally managed to reach San Gallo, if he did not give up the long trail in sympathy for his sore feet.

After that, Speedy headed due south, in the hope that he might eventually blunder onto the right way. Otherwise, after reaching the coast, he would have to wander up it until he found the house and the lagoon.

So he came down into the coast country, a land of chaparral with thorns like the claws of a tiger, cactus, pale-gray mesquite, a gray land, covered with sun-cured gray grass, pale with dust. Even the live oaks were gray with a draping of the sad Spanish moss. Small, tough cattle, wilder than deer and savage as beasts of prey, grazed those miles. Sometimes Speedy saw them cantering with a long, stretching lope. He knew what that meant, and followed. He could see more and more of the cattle coming from several directions, aiming at a focal point. That point was a big stretch of stagnant water, a tank made by building a costly dam of masonry across the course of a creek, and so saving the winter rains for the drought of summer.

To that artificial lake, the cattle had to come from a great distance. All around it, the grass was eaten to the roots for a mile, and, having watered, the wise range cattle went back again, at a trot or a gallop, steering for some distant grassy sections. For two days, three days, even four days, some cowpunchers swore, those steers would remain grazing on the dry, acrid grass before the need of water sent them back, red-eyed, toward the tank.

Numbers of them were in the water, belly-deep, or lying down near the verge of the lake waiting until they could take a second or a third drink, before turning back once more toward their chosen grazing land. Myriads of sea birds, regardless of the beeves, covered the face of the lake, but they rose with a roaring of wings when they saw Speedy come near.

He rode into the lake, over the hard-caked and cracking ground from which the water had retired, over the soggy mud of the border, and then well out into the tank. When he paused, the animals nosed the stale water once or twice, shook their heads in protest — and then drank deeply.

Speedy was pleased. Mules are not dainty, but a horse that consults necessity rather than individual taste is the horse for the Southwestern desert. Looking over that ill-smelling lake, he felt the grimness of the country more than ever. What would have been an abomination in luckier land was a treasure here. The cattle came to it. So did the beasts of prey.

He saw the trail of a jaguar, the immense print of the forepaw clearly marked on the soft mud at the edge of the water. A puma had been there, little wildcats had come down to lap the warm water, and deer, and hogs, and there were the tiny hoof marks of the peccaries. All of these signs overworked by the complicated patterning where the sea birds had walked. One tragedy was there. The carcass of a dead beef showed on the edge of the water, where the soft mud had pulled down some thirst-starved beast that stood still for too long, and let the muck underneath imprison its legs.

Speedy rode on. It was very hot. The heat waves that reflected from the surface of the earth made the air tremble. Only now and then the blue water of a mirage shone steadily as a sapphire in the distance. But Speedy was not tempted. Those fair visions, he knew, were too beautiful for the country that embosomed them.

The sun was still well up in the sky, when he came to a hill that was reasonably high for the midst of that low rolling or level country. He climbed it. At the top there was the outline of a trench that had been dug, and an embankment thrown up outside it. Men had been besieged here, perhaps 100 years ago. Perhaps, here, the natives had surrounded a little party of armored Spaniards and held them while the sun did the work of death better than arrows could have managed it.

From that height, Speedy looked far out to the coast, and to the dull sheen of the sea beyond. He saw the wavering coastline, with one deep lagoon stuck like a silver dagger into the heart of the land, and a house at the end of it.

That was San Gallo, he could be sure. It was not forty miles, after all, and the big horse was still fresh enough.

Through that clear air, he could see to a vast distance; he could mark the form of a horseman on a low sand dune near the injutting lagoon. He could see the piers of the old wharf, which looked like the upstanding teeth of a broken comb. All of this was very small and fine, something to be squinted at and guessed rather than seen. But very real was the new ozone that he breathed, the sweet and dangerous air of adventure.

For that was the port to which Isabella, who had escaped, was coming in a sailing vessel. Was she old or young? *Young*, said the heart of Speedy. Who was Materro, who had signed the cablegram? Was it he who had imprisoned Isabella?

There was enough in the air to have made another man turn back, but Speedy began to sing. He tapped a big canvas saddlebag, and the strings of the guitar gave out a soft chord of accompaniment.

But there were preparations to be made. He might need a new identity in San Gallo.

So Speedy dismounted, took the roll from behind the saddle, and unfurled it. He shed his own clothes and gleamed for an instant in the flash of the sun like a ruddy bit of bronze, striped about the hips with white.

Out of the roll he took a pair of corduroy trousers, much too large for him, and with the bag in them coming down halfway between his knees and his ankles. He put on the trousers, a ragged blue flannel shirt, and a plaid vest into which two bodies as large as his own could have been slipped. He girded about his neck a tie of flaming crimson, with yellow spots in it, and put on his head a cap that puffed out behind and sloped forward into a very deep visor that made his face seem older and more lean and pointed. He got on his feet a pair of socks, and shoes over them. The uppers of those shoes were badly scuffed and worn, but his feet were fitted perfectly. Only the cleverest of shoemakers could have built those shoes so exactly, and made them so light and so supple between the ball of the foot and the heel. In those shoes a tightrope walker could have performed.

Speedy put away his discarded clothes with care, and did them up in the roll. He carried several changes of outfit with him, for in his life of aimless wandering, when he was led across thousands of miles every year by horse or the iron trail of the railroad, he sometimes needed to change his skin, as it were. For he hunted neither man nor gold, but only the goddess of adventure — a fair face and treacherous eyes for a man to love.

She was not far from him now, he was certain, and that was why he laughed aloud as he sat in the saddle again, and sent the big gelding forward toward the ranch house. He felt that, even if he encountered Tim, he could trust the ragged Mexican asleep in the sun would not be recognized in one who seemed like a Gypsy of the plains.

In a draw he unsaddled the black horse and turned it loose. Then he rode on with the mule.

He saw that the ranch house was a typical one of that section of the country as he drew nearer to it. The kitchen was at one end of the building, the bunkhouse was at the other, and these two extremities were joined by an open-faced hall in which dangled saddles, bridles, and a thousand odds and ends.

Speedy tethered the mule at the hitch rack, and went toward the front door. When he rapped at it, it was opened by a fellow with a concave face that bulged out at the forehead and at the chin. The central section of that face had been mashed flat by the kick of a horse.

The man waited for no questions, but said simply: "No handouts here. On your way, kid," — and slammed the door.

# CHAPTER
# FOUR

A little shudder ran through the body of Speedy as the door crashed before him. It might have been fear; it might have been anger; it might have been an excess of that same eerie emotion that had gripped him when, from the hilltop, he first looked down on the house and the harbor of San Gallo.

He went to the kitchen door, up two steps from the ground, and pushed it open.

"Hello, doctor," he said.

The cook turned slowly, an ominous slowness. He was a big bulk of a man with a swollen red face, and his sleeves were turned up over hairy arms to his elbows, and all his great body was encased in a canvas apron, finger-marked and hand-marked with grease. He looked across his shoulder at Speedy.

"On yer way," said the cook. "You want a hand-out . . . they's a place twenty, thirty mile up the coast where they feed bums."

"This looks all right to me . . . this place," said Speedy. "The place looks all right, and the cook looks all right."

The cook was stirring in a large kettle with a ladle.

"I'll give you a good reason for likin' this place better, kid," he said.

He turned as he spoke, and hurled a dipperful of boiling-hot soup toward the doorway. His viciousness made him swing a little too far. Only half of the liquid passed out the doorway. The other half splattered over the wall, and made the cook shout with rage.

He would have felt much better if he had doused Speedy with scalding soup, but he had seen the stranger side-step like a dancer out of harm's way.

Speedy appeared again, smiling, lifting his deep-visored cap.

"You fellows are a jolly lot down here," he said. "You like your little jokes, eh?"

"Little jokes? Damn you! We like our little jokes, do we?" shouted the cook. "I'll little joke you. Joe! Sailor Joe! Come here!"

"All right!" called a distant voice. A door slammed. Heavy footfalls came near.

"Take that bum by the scruff of the neck and throw him off the place," said the cook.

Sailor Joe was as big as the cook, pound for pound, but there was not a scruple of fat on him. His face was blackened by a beard that would not stay shaved; his brow was blackened by a scowl that would not clear away. Sailor Joe was a brute by nature, and there was so much of him that all the days of his life he had had his way.

When he saw Speedy, Joe laughed loudly, his face twisting crookedly to the side, his mouth sprawling open, his eyes disappearing. Then he strode for the kitchen door — and Speedy.

The latter backed down the steps, not in haste, but pleading as he went.

The cook bawled in a huge voice: "Come on and see the racket, boys! Turn out!"

Promptly three men turned out of the bunkhouse door to see what was going on. One was the fellow with the concave face, one was an elderly cowpuncher, one a chunky bulldog of a brute.

It was the elderly cowpuncher who cried: "What's the matter with the kid? Leave him alone, Joe! He ain't done nothin' but ask for a hand-out, has he?"

"Shut up, Danny," said the fellow with the concave face. "Leave Joe have his way. Kind of time that we let tramps know that they ain't wanted down here. Besides . . ."

The last words were drowned by the first roar of Sailor Joe as he advanced.

Speedy, still retreating, clinging, seemed to realize that he could not flee fast enough to avoid and escape the wrath of Joe. He tried to placate the sailor with words, but Joe, his fury mounting as he saw the chance of resistance diminish, suddenly charged.

He swung for the head of Speedy with all his might, the weight of his great body, the weight of his run all lurching behind the punch. And Speedy seemed to stumble as though fear had weakened his knees. His head swayed under the avalanche of that flying arm. His shoulder struck the ribs of Sailor Joe with a great resounding thwack as Sailor Joe charged on.

It was as though Joe had rammed his ribs against the stump of a tree. He bent over, with a gasp and a grunt, while the men of San Gallo whooped with delight, and Speedy seemed to stagger helplessly away, as though overcome by the impact. He seemed falling, or about to fall, wavering to this side and that, as Sailor Joe charged again, more blindly, with a redoubled force. In fact, the mere wind and coming of that danger appeared to overwhelm Speedy, so that at the last instant he slipped to his hands and his knees.

Sailor Joe tripped on him as on a stone. His arms being thrown out for the purpose of seizing and destroying the smaller man, he was not able to use them to break the fall, and down came Joe with a terrible impact that sounded like a broom smiting a carpet that hangs on a clothesline for the Monday housecleaning. He landed on his stomach and his face, while a dust cloud spurted out on either side of him. His body shook like a jelly, and he lay still.

Speedy, getting to his feet, brushed off his knees, and gaped at the surroundings.

"What happened?" he exclaimed.

Several voices shouted with laughter, at this.

"Joe's corked," said one. "He's all done in by that kid. You fell into some hot luck, kid, is all that happened."

"Luckiest thing that I ever seen," said another, and in his delight he kicked a pebble that sprang to a distance and scattered through a little tangle of tall grass.

Out of that grass slid, instantly, a sinuous shape that flashed in the sun and then coiled — a five-foot diamondback with its head drawn back and its supple neck ready to strike death into any enemy.

Sailor Joe had begun to quiver and writhe as consciousness returned to him — but not breath. He was unregarded in the presence of the snake, however.

"Right here by the house, where a hoss or a man could 'a' been bit!" exclaimed the cook, pulling out a gun.

"Wait a minute!" cried Speedy. "No use in wasting a good snake."

He was rolling up his sleeve as he advanced toward the rattler.

"That snake," he said, "will eat a lot of rats and other vermin, if you don't kill it. Take the poison out of it and let it be, friends."

"You take the poison out of it," said the cook. "Can you do that?"

They began to gather closely around the spot, while Speedy, continuing to roll up his right sleeve, showed a forearm slender enough, to be sure, but rounded and alive with a sinuous interplay of lithe muscles. That arm was something like the body of a snake, the wrist like a snake's supple neck, and the hand like the snake's head, capable of lightning movement.

The diamondback, as though it feared so many huge creatures approaching, turned and fled, but a long, eerie whistle came from the lips of Speedy and stopped it. It coiled. The whistling continued, running through cadences strange and unmusical to all the human ears that heard it, but it seemed to enchant the snake with delight. For the rattler stopped sounding its whirring alarm, raised its head, and began to sway it sinuously from side to side with the rhythm.

Speedy, while he whistled, now held out his hand, and, bending over, he approached the snake little by little.

Sailor Joe had got staggeringly to his feet by this time, still gaping and gasping. He had lost a tooth in that fall. Blood streaked his face and worked in small rivulets through the dust, but he forgot his own pains instantly when he saw the picture of the stranger and the rattlesnake.

"He's inside of the strikin' distance," said Sailor Joe. "He's goin' to catch it."

"Shut up," said the cook breathlessly. "Sure he's in strikin' distance. And he'll get it in a minute, or I'm a fool!"

"I hope," murmured Sailor Joe, "that there snake pours a pint of poison into him, till he swells up and turns black and busts with it."

Only the elderly man, Danny, showed any concern, for he said: "Look out, son. You may be fast, but a snake's a lot faster."

"Leave him be," said Chive, the man with the concave face. "This is the kid's show, and it ain't costin' you nothin' to see it. He's crazy, is what the kid is, and, if the snake kills him, it'll just put him out of pain."

The whistling of Speedy continued, and the undulations of the raised portion of the snake went on until there was a sudden pause in the music. At that instant, the snake struck. But it was a clumsy striking, with only a partial retraction of the head, and a rather aimless flinging forward of the body. Even then, it appeared to the watchers a movement faster than their eyes could follow. But Speedy had followed it both with eye and hand; he shifted suddenly as a dead leaf struck by the wind. The head of the snake struck the ground beside his foot, and instantly Speedy had it gripped about the neck.

The long, brilliant body coiled, at the same time, around the bare forearm of Speedy. A grasp of horror came from every throat. Fascinated, with bulging eyes, those hardy fellows stood around, and watched a knife come into Speedy's hands. He worked, quickly and rather gruesomely with the point and edge of it, in the mouth of that rattler. Presently he flung the snake away from him, and it flashed off like a whiplash into the grass.

"There," said Speedy. "That snake will eat a lot of rats and vermin, now, and it won't kill anything too big for it to swallow. Snakes and owls do a lot of good, they tell me."

"Where'd you learn that trick?" demanded the cook.

"Old tramp taught me," said Speedy. "You pick up a lot of things on the road, if you keep your eyes and ears open."

"I've seen you before," said the cook. "Where?"

"I don't know," said Speedy. "Going by on the top of a train, maybe, or on the back of a good, fast mule."

The men laughed again at this.

"And where'd you learn to fall down and trip gents like that?" boomed Sailor Joe, reaching for the shoulder of Speedy.

32

He clutched the thin air, for Speedy had withdrawn a half step, saying: "I'd like to get some soap and water to wash the snake off my skin."

"Maybe the snake's more under your skin than on it," suggested Joe savagely.

"Let him alone," said the cook with authority. "The kid's earned a hand-out. I never seen such a thing in my life. Take charge of him, Danny. Chive, stay out here. I gotta talk to you about something."

# CHAPTER
# FIVE

They walked up and down — the man with the battered, concave face, and the cook — while the latter asked: "Whatcha think of that kid? Seems like I've seen him somewhere."

"If I'd ever seen him . . . at work," said Chive, "I'd sure remember him."

"I never seen him at work," said the cook, "but I've seen him somewhere, seems to me. Something about him . . . it kind of struck inside of me. Maybe it was a long time ago. Seems like it was a younger kind of a face that I remember. How old would he be? Twenty-two?"

"Nigher to twenty-four," said Chive.

"Sure was funny, the way Joe happened to fall all over him."

"There wasn't any happen to it," said Chive.

"Whatcha mean by that?" asked the cook calmly.

"I mean what I say."

"You mean that the kid done all those things on purpose?"

"That's what I mean."

"Come along," said the cook. "You dunno what you're talkin' about. Joe could break him to bits, and the kid knew it, and he was so scared that he fell of a heap, was all."

"He seem scared to you?" said Chive.

"Well, didn't you see his eyes, the way they bugged out, and the way he begged Joe to leave him alone? Scared? I never seen anybody more scared."

"You can make your eyes bug out, and you can make yourself talk fool talk," said Chive. "But you can't change the color of your face. And his face didn't change none. A man that's real scared gets white around the mouth and in the middle of the cheek. He might not change any other place, but he gets white there. But the kid didn't get white no place at all. I took a look . . . see, and I seen."

"You're just nacheral suspicious," said the cook. "The kid just had a flock of luck, was all. He was scared to death, I'd say."

"All right," said Chive, "but lemme tell you something. When you tackle that kid, you tackle him with a gun. And you'd better be sure to get the drop, because if he's fast with a Colt as he is with a snake, he'll shoot the middle piece out of you before you get your gun talking."

"He was pretty slick with that snake," said the cook, agreeing slowly. "But you're wrong about the rest. He's got a wide-open eye. There ain't any meanness at all in him."

"A lot of females have wide-open eyes, too," said Chive, "and them are the kind that do you in, old son. Remember that. Suppose that this kid is just a nacheral-born actor, eh?"

"I'll take my chance," said the cook, shrugging his big shoulders. "Now listen to me. I got something more to talk about than snake charmers. I wanna know how things are goin'."

"None too good," Chive said. "I try to keep the boys lined up. But it's a hard job. I'm mighty respectful to Lew Crocker, all the time, and I work hard to keep the boys lined up, but they're apt to get sassy. They know damn' well that they're gettin' their extra money from Tim and Steve. And, of course, that makes them back-talk to Lew Crocker a good bit."

"The fools," said the cook furiously. "They'll spoil everything."

"That's what I've told 'em," said Chive. "I've told 'em twenty times that what they're to do is to pretend to be real, honest cowpunchers and pull the wool over the eyes of Lew Crocker . . . until the right time comes. But it's a rough lot that Steve got together here."

"Look here . . . is young Crocker gettin' suspicious?"

"He is," said Chive. "He'd 'a' fired the whole bunch of 'em, except for me talkin'. As cowpunchers, they're a pile of hams, these fellows. Sailor Joe can't handle any end of a rope, and the whole bunch are lazy and mean. They've lived by their guns too long. I could talk Lew Crocker out of being suspicious, though, if it wasn't for old Danny. He keeps an eye out. He works hard as the devil himself, and he's always out on the range where he can tell how these mugs are wastin' their time. He reports to Lew Crocker, and Lew gets hot. But he's a decent young gent. He's patient, and he tries to believe me when I tell him that they're goin' to work into shape and be the best gang of cowhands on the range. He's a pretty good sort, Lew Crocker is. You gotta hand it to Lew for the way he's taken hold of this ranch and kept it going after his old man died."

"Listen to me," said the cook.

"I'm listening," said Chive.

"Get over this idea of being fond of Lew Crocker. Who's paying you the real money? Or are you working for Crocker's fifty a month?"

"Damn the fifty a month," said Chive. "I know who I'm workin' for. I was only talking, was all."

"All right. It's time to quit the talking and get to work," said the cook.

"You mean . . . what?"

"Where's Lew Crocker now?" asked the cook.

"Rode down to the lagoon, I guess. Spends some time every day down there by the old harbor. Maybe he's got an idea that he's goin' to fix it up into a little port, once more, to ship the cattle out."

"He ain't goin' to ship no cattle, and he ain't goin' to make no port," said the cook calmly. "The reason he's down there, every day, is because he's gone and got word that something he wants is likely to come into sight off that lagoon."

"Is that why he's built the rowboat?" said Chive.

"Sure it is. But he ain't goin' to row in that rowboat. I think the time's nearly come for him to die, Chive."

Chive started violently. He darted a hand up to his misshapen face, and lowered it again. His eyes were large, but gradually they began to narrow.

The cook, who was watching him closely, said: "You like this kid, eh?"

"I like him, but I like five hundred bucks a whole lot better," said Chive.

"There's goin' to be more than five hundred in this for each of us," said the cook. "There's more to this job than you think. Killing Lew Crocker is only a start, maybe. I've heard Steve do a little talking."

"About what?" asked Chive.

"About things that I can't talk about yet, but I know there's a big deal in the background, if only all the boys stick with Steve and Tim. You're a gent that they could count on, Chive. I've always knowed that."

"What'll we do with old Danny?" said Chive.

"There ain't enough blood in him," answered the cook, sneering, "to make a good-sized stain on the floor."

"Can't we send him away some place?" asked Chive.

"So's he could give evidence?" said the cook. "Matter of fact, Chive, the way I see this business is that old Danny goes off his nut and pulls a gun, and shoots his boss dead, and, while Lew Crocker is fallin', he shoots Danny full of holes. And there you are with a story to tell any sheriff that happens along."

"Steve and Tim have done a lot of talking to you," suggested Chive.

"Yeah, here and there," said the cook.

"You got brains," admitted Chive, nodding his head very seriously as he looked at the other.

"All cooks have got brains. They've *got* to have them," said the cook.

"When does the shooting come?" asked Chive.

"Any day," said the cook, "when Tim or Steve get back and give the word."

# CHAPTER
# SIX

Where we find kindness, we are inevitably lured to expect and believe in honesty, also. As for Speedy, those swift, accurate eyes of his had already read the faces and in part the minds of the men of San Gallo. Chesty, the little bulldog, Chive, the scarred and savage warrior, the two brutes, the cook and Sailor Joe, had all been sifted and appraised by Speedy. They looked to him like a gang of thugs. But Danny was a different metal. He was over fifty, yet still hardy. Time had drawn his face and picketed his eyelids, but it had not yet dimmed his gray eyes. His expression was sour enough, but his speech was drawling and very kind.

He had shown Speedy where to put up the mule, and they walked back toward the house slowly together.

"Things seem pretty peaceful down here," said Speedy. "I don't suppose that anybody would ever have to run for it, down here, unless the sea rose and came pouring in. Or do you have to fight rustlers, or something like that? Looks like you have a hand-picked gang of gunmen, Danny."

Danny looked sharply at him, pausing. The sun slid under the western rim of the sky, and the broad-banded colors began to sweep the heavens.

**40**

"Well," said Danny, "they may be gunmen, but I didn't pick 'em."

He scowled down at the ground.

"They look to me," said Speedy, "good enough for a murder any day."

Again the head of Danny twitched as he looked suddenly straight at Speedy.

"What you got on your mind?" he asked.

The glance of Speedy had not been so openly aware of his companion, but, nevertheless, he had looked into the very mind of the cattleman, and he felt that he could place some trust here. They were all of one cut, those other fellows; Danny was a different stripe. Perhaps Danny would fall in the slaughter.

He fumbled for guidance with his next words.

"Nothing on my mind, much," said Speedy. "Is this the whole layout? This the whole crowd, that I've seen?"

"All except the boss," said Danny. "And the Lynches."

"Yeah? And what's the boss like?"

"Lew Crocker? He's as clean a cut as you ever seen, is what he's like. A dog-gone' upstanding boy, and a good head too."

We rarely praise honesty in others unless we are honest ourselves. There was a certain heartiness in these words that won the trust of Speedy more profoundly than before.

"Young, clean-cut, upstanding," murmured Speedy. "It's a queer thing, Danny, that he'd go in for a crew like this."

"Six weeks ago we had a different outfit," said Danny gloomily. "We had men that had been here for a long time, most of 'em. And then things started happening. Couple of 'em got into a fight in town, up in Porto Nuevo. They got cut up pretty bad, and we had to have a new pair, and the first that the boss picked up was Steve Lynch . . . his brother Tim fills in, sometimes . . . and Chive, the gent with the busted face.

"The end of the month, two more of the boys stepped out of the picture. Seems they got boiled and left Porto Nuevo and didn't come back, or something, and one of them was cook, so we got the new cook and Chesty, and that's the way it's gone. Seems like the gents at Porto Nuevo are layin' for the 'punchers from San Gallo, and it just happens that every time, lately, that we lose a good 'puncher, we get a gent that looks like a yegg to take his place. Just had luck, I reckon. And they're bad cowhands, too, lemme tell you."

"Well," said Speedy thoughtfully, "when a crowd is not all of one kind, there's apt to be trouble."

"Aye," said Danny warmly, "there's apt to be trouble. They ain't my kind, none of 'em. They give me the cold shoulder. And they ain't Lew Crocker's kind, neither. And that makes trouble. The boss is getting sort of grouchy at 'em. Not that some of 'em don't work hard. There's Chive. He's a good cattleman. He knows his business, and he works mighty hard. So does Steve Lynch, and Tim, when he's here."

As they came back into the bunkhouse, they found that the other men had gathered there.

42

Speedy said, quietly, as he came through the door behind Danny: "Well, when I feel bad weather in my bones, I keep my eyes open. You'd better do the same."

That was all that he ventured to say. It won him a curiously piercing glance from Danny, but Lew Crocker came in a little later, and the cook beat a gong to announce supper.

Lew Crocker was a fellow worthy of note. Sun-browned, lean, stalwart, he was as fine-looking a man as Speedy had seen in many a league of wandering, and he had the clean, clear eye of a man who has no shadows on his soul. That surety came to Speedy as he sat down at the foot of the table, opposite to Danny, and saw the master of the house at the head, speaking cheerfully to his men. The joy of life and strength of youth was in him. He was not many years past twenty, and life as yet had not marked him except to place the one wrinkle between his eyes, the brand of labor and its pain.

What Speedy wanted, above all, was a chance to talk for two minutes alone with Crocker. In those two minutes, it might be hard to convince him of the extent of the danger that was threatening him, and its reality, but Speedy felt that the warning must be given soon.

Tim Lynch was not a fellow who would be permanently held up by the difficulties of the way, or by the lack of a horse. He was the sort of a man who seemed capable of going on his own way in one manner or another. And Tim at any moment might arrive.

That was why the need of Speedy for speech was very great, but he had to talk in private. He could not call Crocker to the side without awakening suspicions in the others, and Speedy had reason to feel that the rest of the gang were well primed for action of any sort. The very way in which Chive and some of the others looked at the boss was proof that they were ready for action.

Yet there was no chance to talk before supper. Lew Crocker himself led the way, and, although Speedy tried to hurry up to him, he failed. There began for him a long and nervous agony of strain, while he searched his brain for an opportunity to convey his warning.

It was a good supper. You can judge a rancher, very often, by his willingness to feed his men well. And with that as a criterion, young Crocker appeared a very fine master, indeed. *Frijoles* there were, of course, that far south. And there was roast beef, and a strong soup, and heaps of fried potatoes, and stewed corn, and hot bread. The cook was an artist, in his way, and, although he scowled at Speedy every time he entered the room, he could be forgiven. All cooks have bad tempers — that is a legend and a truism in the West.

There was not much conversation, although at one moment it touched on Speedy.

"You strange to this part of the world?" asked Lew Crocker.

"I've never been right here before," said Speedy. "But I keep on the wing, a good deal."

"Punching cows?" asked Crocker.

"No, sir," said Speedy. "I've never done that. I juggle a little," he continued, picking up on empty glass, a saucer, and a pair of knives, and making them whirl in twinkling circles into the air as he talked. "And I do a few card tricks. If people want music, I whang a guitar, and sing to please their ears, or I dance to tickle their eyes."

He replaced the articles he had been juggling so skillfully. The sparkling eyes of the men flashed at him as though he were a newly discovered treasure.

"And then," said Speedy, "I'm a mind-reader, particularly when I work with cards or a crystal ball. I tell the future, Mister Crocker. And I pick up a few pennies that way. I'm handy to mend broken pots and pans, too. And I do other odds and ends to pick up a living. I can hook onto a freight car or catch the blind baggage when a train's traveling fast, and I'm at home on the back of a mule. And that's the way I get around the world."

"Other words," said Sailor Joe, "you're just a bum."

"Be quiet, Joe," said Crocker. "He's my guest . . . he's the guest of all of us. And I hear that you charm snakes, too. What's your name?"

"I've been called a lot of names," said Speedy. "Such a heap of them that it would be hard for me to burrow down through the lot and find my real moniker. Some call me Sleepy, and some call me Slow, and some call me Sunshine, because I like to lie in it, and some call me Mississippi, and some call me Speedy . . . because I do little tricks with my hands."

"Speedy," said Sailor Joe, "you ever do an honest day's work in your whole life?"

"Such as what?" asked Speedy.

"Ever work on the street, or in a lumber camp cuttin' wood, or ever haul with a team, or ride range on a ranch, or have a job in a town, or do anything that meant eight or ten hours of drillin' in a day?"

"I'll tell you how it is," said Speedy. "I'm a nervous sort of a fellow. And a very good doctor told me, once, that the best thing in the world for nerves is a change. So I've kept on giving myself one change after another, and I don't really settle down long enough to take up a job of any kind."

The meal was ending. Chive produced a pack of cards, and tossed them to Speedy.

"Lemme see some of this fortune-telling. Start in with my past," said Chive. "Dog-gone me, but I love to show up a faker."

"All right," said Speedy, taking the cards out of the case and pouring them from hand to hand with great adroitness, until they seemed a mere liquid flash in the lamplight. "All I can see is what the cards show me. I'll ask them a few questions."

He shuffled them, and dealt with a rapid flick four cards, all black.

He swept them up with a sudden gesture.

"All dark," he said, shaking his head. "Been anything shady in your life, Chive?"

"What do you mean by that?" asked Chive.

"Well, I didn't stop to ask the cards," said Speedy. "Some fellows are pretty sensitive, Chive, and they don't like to have the cards talk too much about 'em. But we'll see what this hand is saying."

46

He spread them on the board and shook his head over them.

"It looks," he said, "a lot like stripes and bars. A lot like that. Prison . . . or just jail, Chive? No, prison, I'd say. For several years you . . ."

"You crook," said Chive. "Who you talkin' to? To hell with you and your cards!"

But there was a very loud and continued burst of applause from all the rest. Lew Crocker was smiling a little to one side of his face.

Chive stamped off from beside Speedy, but curiosity drew the cook into the same place.

"Never mind about the past," said the cook. "Tell me about the future."

Four diamonds came out of the pack — they seemed, in fact, to come out of the top of it, so expert was the manipulation of those flying fingers.

"Hello," said Speedy, "what sort of a crowd is this? A jailbird . . . asking your pardon, Chive . . . and here's a fellow with a killing in mind. Or what would all of this red mean?"

"Killing?" growled the cook. "I never heard of such a fool idea. Your cards are crazy!"

"They may be crazy," said Speedy, lifting his dark, innocent eyes to the cook's face. "I only tell you what they tell me. Let's see what else they say."

"Oh, the devil with 'em," said the cook. "This ain't fortune-telling. It's just talkin'."

"Try me," said Crocker. "Want me down there?"

"It's better," said Speedy.

Crocker came down and sat on the edge of the table, smiling.

"I want news," said Crocker.

"News about what?" said Speedy. "Money?"

"All right . . . try money," said Crocker.

A mixture of clubs and diamonds fell on the table, face up.

Again Speedy shook his head.

"It looks to me," he said, "as though the cards were saying that you're more likely to lose money, before very long, than you are to win any."

"So?" said Crocker.

"You see how it is," said Sailor Joe. "The poor bum, he thinks people will believe him more if he tells 'em bad news. That's all."

"Try something else," said Speedy carelessly. "Women?"

"All right," agreed Crocker, laughing. "Try that."

Again cards fell.

"Hold on," said Speedy. "I hate to tell you what the cards are telling me. It sounds too much like the usual line of bunk that the Gypsies talk. But . . . you see where the queen lies? As sure as fate, Crocker, a girl is coming to you . . ."

"What sort of a girl?" asked Crocker.

"Dark," said Speedy, half closing his eyes as though in the profoundest concentration. "Black hair and black eyes. And olive skin, but with a flush of color in it."

"By thunder!" breathed Crocker. "And coming to me, did you say? Do you mean traveling?"

48

"Why," said Speedy, "according to the cards . . . and that's why I hate to say it because it sounds so foolish . . . but, according to the cards, the girl is coming to you across the sea."

Crocker leaped from the table to the floor and exclaimed loudly. "It's the most . . ." he began. Then he leaned against the edge of the table once more and said earnestly: "Tell me some more. What's to happen . . . ?"

"To the girl?" asked Speedy.

"Yes, yes! To the girl! Is there . . . is there . . . is there happiness ahead for her, Speedy? Ask the cards!"

Speedy dealt again, saying: "All I can see is what the cards show me, Crocker."

He stared at the fall of the cards and shook his head again.

"Well," he said, "I hate to keep giving bad news, but it looks as though . . . well, it looks as though there's a lot of trouble ahead for her."

"Trouble?" said Crocker very anxiously.

Speedy looked straight up into his face.

"Yes . . . danger," he said. "You see the ace of clubs beside the queen with . . ."

Chive swept up the cards.

"All nonsense," he said.

"What do you mean by doing that, Chive?" demanded Crocker. "How dare you . . ."

"Why, chief," said Chive, "I don't want to see you cut up so bad about the chatter of a young crook with a pack of cards. Better take roulette seriously, than the meanderings of a fortune-teller. But go on and let him jabber, if you want to."

"No," said Crocker. "I'm sorry I spoke like that, Chive."

"Oh, that's all right, chief," said Chive. "I don't blame you for getting sore. Looked like I was being fresh, or something."

"Just for a moment," said Crocker, laughing, "I was rather carried away . . . that was all. Sorry."

He tossed a dollar to Speedy, who caught it dexterously out of the air.

"Bad news or good news," said Crocker, "you hit on some things that may be true. Here's a little silver for you."

"Thanks," said Speedy, and, as he leaned over in rising, his head came close to that of Crocker, and he added in the most careful of whispers: "Guard your life."

They went on into the bunkhouse, again. And Speedy took note that the face of Crocker remained totally unmoved. But as they passed to the end of the room, Crocker said behind him:

"Guard against whom?"

Speedy turned. His lips hardly stirred as he said: "All but Danny."

"You're a singin' and a dancin' man, eh?" said Sailor Joe. "Well, I can sing and I can dance a little myself. Lemme hear what you can do, kid?"

"I'll get my guitar," said Speedy, "and do what I can."

He started for the door, and Crocker remarked that he'd get a breath of air.

Sailor Joe touched Crocker's shoulder.

50

"That Speedy is a hoss thief," he said. "We'd better get him off the place before the night's over."

"Let's hear him sing first," said Crocker, and stepped out into the night.

# CHAPTER
# SEVEN

In the open night, Speedy saw the tall silhouette of a man as he returned from the shed, and the voice of Crocker said: "Speedy?"

"Yes," said Speedy, coming. "It's time for us to talk."

"About what?" asked Crocker. "What's the idea of this? What's in the air? Is it a lot of sham and nonsense?"

"If you'll listen hard, I'll talk fast," said Speedy. "I saw Steve and Tim Lynch talking today. And they were talking murder. I won't tell you all that happened. The main thing is that after a while I heard 'em name the man who's to be killed. And his name is Lew Crocker. Tim Lynch came toward the ranch to do the job. I managed to stop him on the way and steal his horse, but he's coming again, of course. I don't know when he'll arrive."

In the silence that followed, he could hear the harsh breathing of Crocker, who broke out, suddenly: "They're two of the best men I have!"

"Sure they are," said Speedy. "They're the ringleaders."

The moon was sliding up out of the east, lifting a white pyramid of fire above its coming. A deadly light showed the two men to one another.

"Murder!" exclaimed Crocker. "Murder me? They'll get no loot out of me."

"A fellow called Materro wants you put out of the way," said Speedy. "He cabled to Steve Lynch. I saw the cablegram. He said in the cablegram that this is the time to finish."

"Materro . . . Mateo Materro," groaned Crocker, striking the back of his hand against his forehead. "I know there's plenty of devil in him, but he couldn't . . . not murder . . . he couldn't buy a murder . . ."

"No," said Speedy, "maybe this gang of thugs would do the job for fun. Look at the layout. Look at the way they've shifted your old hands off the place, till only Danny's left. Don't you see that it's a plant, and that you're right in the middle of it?"

"Cold murder," whispered Lew Crocker. His breath seemed to be stopped. "Materro. The uncle. It can't be Materro. Not Isabella's uncle!"

"I saw his name signed to the cablegram," said Speedy. "Don't you see the lay of the land? Materro fixed Steve and Tim Lynch a long time ago. They've managed to run your old hands off the place. They've got the bag fixed and stretched for you, and they're ready to drop you in now. Isn't it as clear as day? Now there is a girl on the way . . . Isabella. She's expected here, and Materro knows it. Don't you see that all the leaders are in place and that you're to be toppled over?"

"Whether I can understand it or not, I've got to see it," said Crocker. "But you, man. What brought you into this? If what you say is true, there's murder in the air. What brought you into it?"

"The odd chance," said Speedy, "plus a little kicking about, and the fact that I can read lips a bit. There's no time to talk of that. What's your plan?"

"To send to town for help," said Crocker. "I've got to get half a dozen men I can trust, and then I'll back the thugs off the ranch."

"That's one way," said Speedy. "I could ride to town for you and choose the men."

"Aye," said Crocker, "and that's the best way."

"Suppose that they find that I'm gone?" said Speedy. "I couldn't be back here before some time tomorrow evening, at the earliest. Suppose that they grow suspicious after I've left and attack you and Danny?"

"That's a chance that I'll have to take," said Crocker.

"Why?" argued Speedy. "There are four of 'em, all told. You and I can sneak into the kitchen and stick up the cook. When we've bundled him up helplessly, then we can go to the bunkhouse, wake up Danny, and try our luck. If the gang wants fighting, we can fight, till they're licked. It's the best way, Crocker. The odds will only be four against our three. But if I rode off, they're likely to grow suspicious, and bump you off and take care of Danny without waiting till I get back. We'd better arrange the showdown right now."

He could dimly see that Crocker was shaking his head slowly. There seemed to be no fear in him; there was simply a calm decision that he was making at the moment.

"There's no chance of winning that way," he said. "Danny's no good with a gun. Neither am I. I've been too busy working, all my life, to spend any time

54

hunting. I can't hit the side of a barn with a rifle, and I'm no good at all with a revolver. I never pack one, as a matter of fact. All the crowd know that Danny and I are pretty useless with guns. They'd simply concentrate on you, Speedy, if a fight began. And after they'd riddled you, they'd take up the work on Danny and me. No, a showdown is no good."

"You're right," said Speedy quietly. "If that's the case, a showdown's no good. Then there's a next best bet. You and Danny and I should slide out of the ranch, go to town, get reinforcements, and come back here to clean up Tim and his crowd."

Crocker pointed out toward the lagoon. It shimmered like silver under the moon, and beyond it was the sea, like a dull, purple mist.

"She may come tonight, Speedy," he said. "I can't leave this place while there's a chance that she may come."

"If she comes . . . But, man," said Speedy, "I saw the cablegram from Materro that says she's not to reach here until between the Tenth and the Twentieth. And the Tenth is not till tomorrow."

Crocker shook his head again.

"Crocker," said Speedy, "this is life or death that I'm talking to you."

"I know it," said Crocker. "I wish that I had words to tell you how I thank you for throwing in with me, Speedy. I haven't the words. But, after thanking you, I'll have to tell you that I'd rather die . . . ten times over . . . than be away from this place if she comes. I can't go."

Speedy stared at him through the dim light, and wondered. He had seen men in love before this, but he felt that he never before had encountered such quiet and manly resolution. There was no passion in the voice of Crocker. There was simply endless resolution.

Speedy argued no more. He merely said: "Have it your own way. I'll take a horse and start back for town. If you can live through sixteen hours or twelve hours with these thugs, I'll be back with help. So long, Crocker."

"If you go," said Crocker, "the place is stripped to Danny and me. Couldn't I get hold of Danny to make the trip? He's in the bunkhouse now. I'll call him out."

"Wait," said Speedy. "They might begin to grow suspicious then. Besides, they're waiting for me to do a song and dance in the bunkhouse. They might suspect something if I don't show up for that. I'll do the song and dance, Crocker, and, while I'm making noise, you find your chance to talk to Danny and to send him off. As soon as the rest turn in, he could slip off and start."

"You're right. You're always right," said Crocker. "If I'm sure of anything, it is that heaven sent you down here. I'm no good at chattering promises and thanks, but if there's blood in me, I'll show you just what I feel before the end of me."

They went on into the bunkhouse together. Danny was in a corner, laying down his blankets. In another corner, Chive, Chesty, and Sailor Joe were in serious consultation.

To warn Crocker, Speedy had gone further, he felt, than he should have done in the fortune-telling. He had

56

exposed too much of his hand. Therefore, his next desire was to dance and sing all seriousness out of the minds of these men. He came into that long, ugly room pirouetting and prancing, and, throwing the cover off the guitar, he struck up a lively tune on it.

Before he had done ten phrases of the piece, the frowns had vanished.

Then he stood panting in a corner and challenged Sailor Joe to show forth his wares.

"I can do a hornpipe and a jog," said Sailor Joe, "but I ain't got wings hitched to my heels, like you have, and I ain't working in the same room. Hit it up, kid, and let's see you prance."

So Speedy pranced.

He showed them how a cat walks across wet ground, while they yelled with delight; he showed them a chicken whirling in great distress when a hawk hovers over the hen and her brood; then he was the hawk itself, hovering, sweeping, sailing through the sky. And he was a lame dog trailing a leg over rough ground; he was a fat man waltzing a German waltz; he was an affected young girl, passing a group of youths on the street; he was as old woman with her arms full of packages that continually fell.

He passed from one bit of nonsense to another, his feet never still, his guitar thrumming rapidly, steadily convenient tunes for the themes in hand. And the men roared and shouted, and smote one another, and occasionally they threw a coin out onto the floor, and this more and more frequently, for part of the diversion was to note the skill with which the dancer fitted his steps and his subject to the picking up of the money.

Then, as he leaned against the wall, laughing and panting, they swarmed about him, making comments.

Only Crocker was busy, talking with Danny in the farther corner of the room. The face of Danny was turned from Speedy, but he could see the head of the veteran lift, and his shoulders stiffen suddenly.

And then a husky voice sounded at the door, saying: "A fine time all you gents seem to be having."

It was Tim Lynch.

He must have walked in his boots until they cramped and tortured his feet beyond sufferance. They had been dragged off, and various parts of his clothes had been cut up to bind over his feet as gear. The result was that he was literally in tattered rags, and the blood from his chafed feet stained the floor he stood on. Ragged as he was, there was the better chance for the enormous physical strength of the man to show through. And in his face there was the agony of a tortured savage who has stood at the stake and now at last is suddenly free, and among the power of his friends.

With the first words that he uttered, he saw and spotted Speedy. The disguise might have been enough to fool the eye of a man less savagely alert, but the guitar, and the singing which he had heard as he came across the night were, indeed, enough to tell Lynch the truth.

He uttered a wild cry — "The greaser!" — and snatched out his gun. No matter how long the march, Tim Lynch would as soon have parted from a limb as from his Colt revolver. Swiftly he made the move, with the yell of rage still distending his throat and his lips.

Speedy, totally unprepared, his back turned at first toward the door, whirled barely in time to whip out his own gun. That of Lynch already was exploding, and the bullet tore Speedy's weapon from his hand and sent it skidding across the floor.

Speedy himself was instantly in the midst of a swirl of the cowpunchers. They reached for him — it was like grasping at a phantom — and all the while the voice of Tim Lynch was thundering out to them orders to catch the scoundrel and hold him fast for one instant. A half second would be enough.

It was a time to test the nerve of brave men. For Speedy, it was like a wild dance with death. For Lew Crocker, it was facing the ultimate disaster.

He knew, now, that all Speedy had told him was true. He knew that he and Danny were helpless with guns, but that it was a case of the pair of them against all the others, if he wished to intervene on behalf of Speedy.

Yet there was not a moment's hesitation in him. A Colt hung in its holster beside the bed of Danny. Instantly it was in the hand of Crocker.

"Now, Danny, or never," he said through his teeth, and the veteran snatched out a gun at the same moment. He followed forward as Crocker ran into the fray.

"Put up your gun, Lynch! Put up your gun, don't shoot, or I'll make you . . ." shouted Crocker.

Tim Lynch turned from beside the door with a maniacal joy in his eyes.

This was the business he had had in mind; the agony of the march on foot across the desert had sharpened him and hardened him until he was a perfect tool for murder.

"You fool, take what's coming to you!" shouted Lynch. "Chive . . . Joe . . . Chesty . . . this is the time. Blast them to hell!"

And he fired pointblank at Crocker.

Other guns were flashing, Speedy, his hands empty, guns on every side of him, saw Crocker pitch on his face, and Danny go down with a stagger and a slump against a bunk from which he recoiled and fell heavily on the floor. There he lay stretched on his back, his arms flung out crosswise, a horrible stain of red flowing on his head.

Speedy saw that last picture as he ran for his life. They had all swept in from the doorway, during the fighting; now, while the noise of the guns still roared in his ears, Speedy cut back for that exit. He heard Tim Lynch bellowing: "Get the greaser! I'm goin' to kill him if it's the last act of my life. Damn this gun!"

He hurled on the floor a Colt that had jammed, and reached for another man's weapon.

The lintel of the doorway was splintered by two bullets as Speedy raced through it, dodging like a snipe to the right, into the open night.

All about him was the terrible silver clarity of the moonlight, and no possibility of concealment nearer than the trees along the lagoon.

Their guns would find him long before he had managed to reach that shelter.

On the floor of the bunkhouse came the thundering of their feet as they started in pursuit.

So he fled upward, not onward. He simply leaped, caught the low projecting eaves, and swung himself with a mighty heave onto the roof. The sides of it slanted a very little. But the top of it was flat, mud covered over heavy rafters. Onto that flat portion he slithered, and lay still, panting.

The pursuit rushed out into the open night, spread, and came to a stand.

"Where did he go?" called the voice of Sailor Joe. "I wanna get at him. I wanna get at him with my hands. I've gotta get that throat of his under my thumbs . . . and then I . . ."

"Look out in the shed," said Tim Lynch. "Joe, you and Chive look out there."

"He didn't have time to get there," declared Chive.

"What'd' he do, then? Turn into air?" demanded Lynch. "You gents all think you know too much. Go out there and look. Come on back with me, Chesty. We gotta stow the dead ones away in Crocker's room. Too bad that the pair of 'em shot each other up that way!"

And his loud, bawling laughter broke the night.

# CHAPTER
# EIGHT

On the roof, Speedy lay flat on his back and watched the moon ride upward through thin films of clouds. Again he had been beaten. It seemed as though a devil of bad luck pursued him whenever Tim Lynch came on the scene, and now, unarmed, helpless, he had to wait and grimly consult his mind, which would offer no thoughts.

He heard the searchers return from the shed. He heard trampling feet inside the house. At last he ventured down to the ground again. If Crocker and Danny were both dead, perhaps he could purloin a fast horse and ride to bring revengers on the trail. At any rate, he must learn exactly what had happened.

He dropped to the ground and flattened himself in the meager strip of shadow at the base of the well as men came out of the bunkhouse door. He ventured to crawl until he could look around the corner, and he saw three men bearing a loose body with arms that trailed toward the ground.

The head hung loosely, also, and Speedy recognized the face of Danny. His cheeks seemed sunken in against the bone. Under the brows were two pools of such a depth and blackness that the eyes could not be distinguished. It was like the face of a mummy, and the whole body of Danny seemed to be light, as though centuries had dried it.

Chesty carried the head, Sailor Joe had an arm under Danny's hips, and the cook supported the legs. They carried the body down the side of the house and around to the outside entrance of the room of Crocker. Speedy followed like a ghost. He had to crawl with redoubled caution, but he managed to keep close enough.

The three who carried the body talked as they went on.

"Seems like all the weight is drained out of Danny, like all the blood out of a stuck pig," said Chesty.

"Why wasn't this job polished off a long time ago? The killing would've been just as easy a month back," said Joe.

"Where's Speedy?" the cook asked.

"Out lifting himself a fast horse," said Joe.

They came around to the back of the house, where strong lights were shining through the windows of Crocker's room. The door stood open. The yellow lantern light streamed down the steps and died on the brilliant edge of the whiteness of the moonshine. Up those steps, the three carried the helpless body of Danny.

Speedy heard the voice of Crocker exclaiming: "I might have known poor old Danny would be done in at the same time you tackled me! You've murdered him, have you?"

Speedy went to the window, and, looking cautiously over the sill, he saw the whole picture of the interior. The three burden bearers had just dumped the body of Danny, so that it lay face downward. A huge red gash was scored across the head. Crocker, his hands tied behind his back, sat in bloodstained clothes on his bed. He had been shot through the right thigh; big Tim Lynch was bandaging the wound carelessly, pulling the cloth with jerks against the lacerations of the flesh. Chive completed the picture. He walked the floor with a sawed-off shotgun under his arm.

"What's the idea of the bandaging, Tim?" he demanded. "That's just a fool play. Quit the bandaging, will you? Here's Danny flopped on the floor, dead. And there's Crocker, all ready to get a couple slugs of lead in the chest. Why don't you knock him over and then leave 'em lay . . . because they've just killed each other, and that's all that there is to it."

"Maybe there's something more, though," said Tim Lynch, standing up from that roughly completed job of bandaging. He turned his half-handsome and half-brutal face toward Chive. It was plain that the two of them were the leading spirits. The others were hardly more than hired men. "What're we in this for?" asked Lynch.

"Hard cash, brother," said Chive.

"Well," said Tim Lynch, "here's Crocker in a bad pinch. A mighty bad pinch. And Crocker has money in the bank. Quite a lot of money. Maybe he'd like to write us out a check for some of that money. Would we say no to that?"

**64**

He winked at Chive.

Chive answered: "You've got sense, Tim. I didn't think of that. If Crocker's willing to talk business, I suppose that we'd talk business, too."

"Sure we would," said Tim Lynch. He turned back to Crocker. "What you say, brother?" he asked.

Crocker looked at Lynch narrowly.

"I give you a check . . . and what do you give me?" asked Crocker.

"Another chance," said Tim.

"What sort of a chance?" asked Crocker.

"That's a thing for us to figger out," said Lynch.

"Come here," said Chive to Lynch, and drew him back to the window outside of which Speedy was waiting. The murmur of Chive barely reached those eavesdropping ears. "What's the use, Tim? What's the use wasting time? Danny's dead, and we've gotta leave Crocker dead, too. You know that. That's what Materro wants, and he's the big paymaster."

"Never miss an extra dollar, if you have a chance to pick it up," answered Lynch. "And Crocker's willing to talk business. After we get the coin out of him, we can bump him off fast enough."

"Ah, that's the idea, eh?" said Chive.

"Sure. I'm not a fool. Don't it sound good to you?"

"Fair enough. Fair enough," said Chive.

They left the window. Speedy, venturing to look again, saw Lynch go back toward Crocker, saying: "Chive and me, we've agreed. We'll give you your chance, Crocker. But you've gotta pay high for it."

"How high?" asked Crocker.

"You've got more'n ten thousand dollars in the bank," said Lynch.

"Not half that," answered Crocker,

"Well, call it four thousand that you've got," said Lynch.

"Call it that," agreed Crocker.

"You write out your check for that, and we'll give you a break."

"What sort of a break? Turn me loose?"

"Not right away," answered Lynch. "You know that we can't do that."

"I suppose that you can't," said Crocker calmly. His face twisted a little as the pain of his wound pinched him sharply.

Suddenly the loud voice of Sailor Joe boomed: "Look out there! Look!"

Speedy slid back and around the corner of the building in haste. Had they spotted him?

Then he heard Sailor Joe roaring: "Out there on the lagoon! Look!"

Speedy looked, and he saw a two-masted schooner, still blue and dim with distance, standing at the mouth of the lagoon.

# CHAPTER
# NINE

Two of the men strode to a window at once to peer at the vision of the ship. Chive and Lynch continued arguing.

Chive exclaimed: "There's the main bet, right ahead of us! There's our million standing up there on the lagoon like a stack of chips on the plush of a card table. Bump off this fellow Crocker, and get at the big money, Tim."

"Yeah?" drawled Tim. "You talk as though four thousand dollars didn't amount to anything. A day'll come, maybe, when you'll wish that you had a little stake like that four thousand. I'll tell you what, boy . . . it ain't decent to turn down money like that."

"Well," said Chive, "have it your own way and be damned. I don't like this business. Where's that sneaking little juggler of a Speedy?"

"Run away from the guns," answered Tim Lynch. "Likely running now as fast as a hawk. Chesty, you stay here and watch Crocker and Danny. Danny ain't goin' to give you no trouble, and I guess Crocker'll stay put. The rest of us have gotta take a look down the lagoon."

The voice of Chive added: "Keep those eyes of yours open, son. You keep watchin' like a hawk."

"What's there to be scared of?" asked Chesty.

"Shadows . . . hawk shadows slidin' on the ground," said Chive. "Act as though there was a gun pointin' at you all the time."

Then they came swarming out from the house. All went out to the corral to get horses, with the exception of the cook, who hurried around toward the kitchen. His shadow, thrown far forward by the moonlight, gave Speedy his warning. He slipped to the ground and lay face down, praying that the eyes of the cook might not find him.

Heavily trampling feet went by so close that a puff of dust squirted out from under one of them and half choked Speedy. He had to grit his teeth to keep from sneezing; to avoid the sneeze, he almost had to choke himself. But the cook had gone by. The kitchen door slammed, and presently the heavy tread of the cook went off behind the house toward the corral.

A horse squealed in the corral. Hoofs began to trample. Then Speedy saw the shadowy riders, one after another, sweep across the moon-whitened ground and fly off toward the lagoon, and there came the ship, growing on the eye with great slowness, a painted thing rather than a reality.

There was a sudden commotion inside the room of Crocker, a loud shouting from Chesty, and Speedy reached the window in time to see Danny, the supposed dead man, shrunk back against the wall with his hands spread out behind him to secure support, while he stared into the two muzzles of the gun that Chesty held. Blood worked in slow rills down the face of Danny. That he was alive seemed more than a miracle.

"You will, will you?" shouted Chesty. "You'd try to trip me from behind, eh? You'd try to double-cross me, will you, you dirty sneak? Well, you're goin' to get it now. You're goin' to get hell, and I'll be the one to give it to you!"

Speedy reached the doorway, and slipped through.

"Where'll you have it?" said Chesty, his chunky body set swaying with rage and brutal desire. "Body or head? I'm goin' to be a gentleman, Danny, and give you exactly what you want."

Danny raised a hand and brushed some of the blood from his forehead. He sighed.

"Lemme think, a second, will you, Chesty?" he pleaded.

"I ain't goin' to let you do nothing of the kind," said Chesty. "You come along and try to double-cross me, do you? Well, I'm goin' to give you hell for that. Speak up and say what you'll have."

Speedy was close behind now. He took the edge of his palm like the iron side of an axe, and struck Chesty beneath the ear and across one of the big cords that run down the back of the neck. And Chesty spilled sidewise to a hand and knee.

The fighting instinct was still in him, but his body had been numbed by that paralyzing stroke that deadened the nerve centers. His hand could not resist as Speedy pulled the sawed-off shotgun away from him and covered him with it.

"Stand up," said Speedy.

Chesty rose. He was uncertain on his feet, and his white face was knotted with desperation. His hands worked slowly.

"You're sure having bad luck, Chesty," said the victor.

"A lot of dirty sneaks double-crossin' a gent," gasped Chesty. "A lot of crooks . . ."

The irony of these remarks came home even to the dull wits of Chesty. He was silent, then turned at the command of Speedy and allowed his arms to be bound behind his back.

"Danny, how do you feel?" asked Speedy.

"Like a gent that's been in hell and hardly's clear of it yet," said Danny.

"Are your knees soggy?" asked Speedy.

"No. My legs are getting stronger all the time. They bounced a slug off my head . . . I guess that was all."

Danny had set free the hands of Crocker, by this time, and the rancher, ripping away long strips of the sheet, was binding the bleeding head of the older man.

"I've got to stay here with Crocker and keep an eye on Chesty," said Speedy. "Danny, if you think you can do it, you're going to get the best horse on the place and ride for town. Get a dozen men together, if you can. Try to spot the deputy sheriff and have him with the lot. Tell him that there's murder in the air down here. Get your army together, and send 'em down here as fast as they can come. I don't know how many hours it'll take you to get up there, but tell 'em to kill horses all the way back. Every minute that they cut off from their traveling time is going to be saved lives down here,

70

perhaps. Tell 'em that I'm alone, with one of the thugs and a wounded man on my hands. Now, get out and travel."

"He can't do it," said Crocker. "The thing to do is for you to go, Speedy. We can dig ourselves in here, and fight for a while. And you'll get back with help."

"They'll burn you out," said Speedy calmly. "Danny, get on the way."

Danny said nothing at all. He touched the bandages that now tightly bound up his head. Then he gripped the hand of Crocker, and that of Speedy, and stalked from the house.

Crocker stared after him, shaking his head.

"He wobbles from side to side when he walks. What chance has he of getting through to town?" he asked.

"One in three . . . or thirty . . . I don't know," said Speedy. "I only know that that's the only way. Now the rest of us have to get out of the house."

# CHAPTER
# TEN

Of course Crocker could not walk. Chesty, although his hands were tied behind his back, was perfectly able to assist in the carrying of the burden. He walked ahead, while Speedy went behind, supporting the head and shoulders of the wounded man.

They passed in this way out of the house. Far before them, down the pale stretch of the beach, they saw the little flickering figures of the horsemen dip out of view into a hollow and rise again. Chesty groaned at the sight of his friends.

They went on toward the trees that filled the marsh at one side of the lagoon. Their footfalls *crunched* noisily upon the sand. They seemed the only bit of reality in the midst of a dream of which the most visionary part was that apparition of blue-white sails, entering the mouth of the lagoon.

They reached the trees, a ragged forest draped everywhere with the gloomy Spanish moss. Sometimes they walked in darkness, but with spots of moonlight ahead, to show them the way. Then the sleek, black face of marsh water stopped them. Fallen branches underlay the water like dead snakes, or lifted their ends like watching heads. The scent of decay and slime was sour in the air.

They skirted the water. Beyond it, they reached a small opening in the woods, and here Speedy halted the party. With great tufts of the moss and ends of branches, he made a comfortable bed for Crocker, who relaxed on it with a groan.

Speedy watched over him for a moment, while Chesty was saying: "You gents are crazy. You can't get clear. You're stuck here. It's goin' to take you days to get Crocker well. And Danny'll never reach town to get help. He was too near sunk when he left. The thing you oughta do is to go out and surrender to the boys. They'll give you a good break."

"Are you feeling better?" asked Speedy of Crocker.

The latter raised himself on one elbow, and nodded. Speedy gave him a Colt revolver that he had taken from Chesty.

"Keep Chesty under the muzzle of that gun," said Speedy. "If we were practical men, we'd tap him over the head and slide him into the marsh, but that sort of a short cut to safety doesn't appeal to me. Does it to you?"

"No," said Crocker. "There's no use punishing one hound when the whole pack is at fault. Are you leaving me, Speedy?"

Speedy pointed through the trees.

"I've got to get out there," he said. "I don't know what I can manage, but I've got to try to get to the girl, Crocker."

The body of Crocker lay stretched out in the shadow, but moonlight fell upon his head, and his face puckered with wonder as he stared at Speedy.

"What sort of a fellow are you?" he asked huskily. "I've never raised a hand for you, partner. And you've never seen the girl. There are four thugs who'll shoot you on sight and . . . heaven bless you for anything you can do."

"Don't thank me," said Speedy. "You know how some gamblers are. When they're broke, they'll play for matches. And this is a game for something more than money. So long. Watch Chesty. Watch him like a hawk. If he gets away, the game's lost."

Chesty said nothing at all. His big block of a head was turning slowly from Crocker toward Speedy, and back again. Amazement set in his eyes. He was seeing and hearing matters of which his own native common sense never had warned him before. Imagine someone who was capable of doing something for nothing.

Speedy was already withdrawing, and, once out of sight of the other two, he set off at a rapid run that carried him out of the trees — skirting the foul margin of another marsh — and onto the moon-crisped whiteness of the beach.

Well before him, he saw the schooner drifting inland, with wrinkles in her sails.

He ran on the verge of the water, where the sand was hardest, until he was fairly up to the spot on the shore toward which the ship seemed to be heading. Then he cut inland. The sand was at once softer underfoot. He labored through it with a sound like swishing water about his feet.

So he came through a wilderness of small sand dunes upon sight of the ship and the four men of San Gallo.

It was a natural cover, framed in outjutting rocks, toward which the schooner had headed, and there Tim Lynch and the cook and Sailor Joe and Chive stood beside their horses, waiting. And there was a fifth horse as well — a big brute, with the moon glinting over the silk of its flanks.

The anchor was dropped by the schooner. The cable *clinked* noisily for a moment, then stopped its noise as the anchor struck the bottom through that shallow water. Presently a boat dropped over the side. A crew appeared in it. Oars were thrust out. Like a great insect, the skiff walked across the still surface of the lagoon.

Tim Lynch ran forward to meet it. He stood on the verge of the sea. He waded in, and caught the prow, and drew it up on land.

All of this was seen by Speedy as he lay behind a wide-armed cactus, at times lifting his head to see more clearly through the branches the maneuvering of men and oars.

Most of them were ashore now. And then he saw a hooded form, a slender thing, arise from the stern sheets of the boat.

That was the woman. That was this Isabella Materro who had ventured to love a *gringo*, who had escaped from her rich uncle, who had fled across the sea to find young Crocker. Because of her, two men, already, were wounded. Because of her, a stricken man was urging a horse toward the town to get help. Because of her, perhaps men had died before, and perhaps they would die again.

*Money and women . . . the roots of all evil.* That was the phrase that continually rang in the mind of Speedy as he lay there in the sand and watched.

A *mantilla* cloaked the head of the girl and shrouded her face from him, as she walked up the beach. The captain of the schooner went with her. One could tell that he was a seafaring man by his swaggering walk, by the scuffing of his feet through the sand. One could tell that he was used to command, by his outer bearing. Even the moonlight showed the darkness of his face, tanned by many storms and the keen sun of the open sea.

They came closer. First, Speedy glimpsed the features of the girl. Then he could see her clearly, and he knew that it was right for men to fight and die for her. That face that a man's hand could span, and that would wrinkle with time, and glow leathery with age, was still like music to the soul. A trumpet sounded to the heart of Speedy. He smiled, as he lay there stretched in the sand. His labor was rewarded — all that he had done, and all that he might do. She was not for him. Another man loved her, and another man had won her love. But as the *mantilla* slipped back and the moonlight struck upon her face, he thought that he saw that courage and simplicity and goodness for which men are willing to die.

Tim Lynch was beside them, taking the lead in all the talk.

76

"Crocker couldn't come down," he was saying. "Lew has a touch of the fever. Nothing bad. But the doctor says that he can't show himself to the night air. So he's in bed, but he's seen the ship through the window, and he's waiting. Had to pretty nigh tie him down to keep him from comin' out here."

"A fine kind of a man," said the sailor. "A fine kind of a man that wouldn't drag himself out of the grave to come to this kind of a girl that's come to him out of I dunno what kind of a hell. A fine kind of a man, ma'am," he added to the girl. "I'd do some second thinkin', if I was you. I'd do it before I leaped."

She turned to the captain and lifted her face with a faint smile as though she would not venture to put into words all the faith and the confidence that she felt.

He saw that smile and shook his head. Speedy saw it, also, but he did not smile. There was something deeper than smiles in his gleaming eyes.

She was merely pressing Tim Lynch to learn whether or not Crocker were seriously ill. English was not altogether familiar on her tongue. She spoke it clearly enough, but with a certain drawling, a slowness that made the words more musical. Lynch declared that Crocker was only to be in bed for a few days.

"I'll tell you what," insisted the captain of the schooner, "I don't like the sound of this here. It seems to me like Crocker ain't burnin' up to get his eyes on you. I'm goin' to go along and see this thing through. You don't know these folks. I won't deliver you till Mister Crocker signs on the dotted line."

Inwardly Speedy blessed the resolution of that big fellow.

"Come along, then," said Tim Lynch, with a calmness that he could not be feeling. He might dispose of the captain, to be sure, but there would remain the crew of the schooner and murder on a large scale confronting Lynch and his friends. A little more insistence on the part of the captain, and the whole plot of Lynch would be exposed.

But then a sailor called in Spanish from the skiff to say that a good wind was coming off the shore. It was true. The moonlit bay was darkened by the breeze. The schooner heeled well over with it. There was a *clashing* and *clattering* of odds and ends adrift on the ship as it swayed.

The captain faltered. It was the girl herself who pressed him to go, and finally took his arm and went laughing back with him to the skiff. She told him that she knew she could trust the first men she met on the American shore. There was nothing but happiness and faith in her.

The captain took hold of both her hands, finally, and said good bye.

"D'ye understand?" he said. "You may be the queen of the land with all the money in it, but I feel as if I'm goin' off leavin' you on an island with nothin' but natives around."

Speedy heard her thanking that honest sailor, and saw the skiff push off, and go pacing away like a six-legged water insect toward the schooner. Speedy himself was in an agony. For yonder in that boat,

**78**

hurrying away from him, were men enough to save both the girl and Crocker, if their power was properly used.

But how could it be used?

If Speedy cried out, he would be blown to pieces by the concentrated fire of Lynch and the other three. In fact, those four armed men could master Speedy and the sailors, too, if there were a sudden showdown. The whole balance of power was in their hands, in their guns.

If only a calm would imprison that ship in the lagoon — if only some miracle could enable Speedy to send his thoughts swiftly into the mind of the skipper.

So, in shuddering suspense, Speedy saw the skiff reach the side of the schooner. Already the crew had begun to walk the anchor up from its holding ground; the capstan grunted and groaned with the labor. The small boat was hoisted on board. And now the wind filled the big bellies of the sails and sent the schooner swiftly and smoothly out to sea.

# CHAPTER
# ELEVEN

There is no bewilderment greater than that of the clever man when he feels that he has allowed a great opportunity to slide through his hands, unused. And that was the feeling of Speedy as he saw the ship and its men pass away from the lagoon. Help had been at hand, almost within touching distance, and he had not been able to use it; he had thought of no way of calling those latent powers into action on his side — and yet he was a man of a thousand devices.

He ground his teeth as he lay there in the sand behind the big cactus. He could think now of what he should have done. He should have stolen farther down the lagoon, and slipped into the water unheeded, and then he should have swum out to the schooner, lying on his back, working his arms very carefully so as to raise hardly a ripple. In that way he might have gained the ship and there he could have taken measures to warn the crew of the crime that was about to be attempted on the shore.

He could have attempted that thing, but he had thought of it too late. Now he had to lie there, helpless, while he saw the girl come back with Tim Lynch from the waterside. In spite of the captain's direct warning, she seemed incapable of suspicion, and she was smiling up at Tim with a perfect trust as she walked along with him.

That smile made the resolution of Speedy a thing of steel.

More trouble was coming. Down the beach, from the direction of the house, came the figure of a man, running hard, a short chunk of a fellow. He called out, and waved an arm. It was Chesty, who panted, as he came up: "Tim! Chive! Look out! The devil's loose!"

"What devil? Whatcha mean? Shut up, you fool!" cried Tim Lynch, and looked over his shoulder with guilty fear toward the outline of the disappearing ship.

Chive, who was standing beside the big horse, helping Isabella Materro to mount, also turned with a start, toward Chesty, who panted: "Speedy! He come back! He got Crocker out of the house. Over into the woods by the marsh . . ."

"Shut up, you blockhead!" shouted Tim Lynch. "Scatter out, boys. See . . . The devil take Speedy!"

The girl, as she sat in the saddle now, looked with great, startled eyes toward the men around her. Broken as the words had been, it must have been plain to her, by this time, that there was something very wrong indeed.

Chive and Tim Lynch were springing for their saddles. The cook and Sailor Joe were already mounted, when Speedy slipped from behind the cactus and dashed for the girl, his black shadow sweeping over the ground beside him.

He gained the back of that horse like a panther, and, as he slid into place behind the cantle, his left arm shot past the girl and caught the reins out of her hand; his right hand held his revolver.

But all that courage and address could not have saved the life of Speedy then. The last moment of all his adventures would have come, except that the big horse, leaping wildly away as it felt the impact of that unexpected rider, crashed straight into the mustang that Chive was mounting.

The mustang went down, rolling against the legs of the big gelding on which Tim Lynch was seated. The second horse staggered, almost fell. Even so the bullet from the gun of Lynch clipped hair from the head of Speedy.

But they were through the first pinch. The frightened horse was running like a deer over the firm sand at the water's edge, and the voice of Tim Lynch was yelling to his other men not to shoot. Even at twenty yards the danger of striking the girl would be too great, and her life, not her death, was what they wanted.

It was Lynch who was shouting that one horse could not carry two people to safety. The galloping animals poured after Speedy in a rush, and, looking back, he groaned with relief to see that they were not gaining.

The girl had not screamed out; she had not struggled to escape from the saddle; it would almost have been better had she done so. But what actually happened was that fear had struck her like a club, and now she swayed helplessly to the side, a lurching weight against the arm of Speedy. He, without stirrups under him, without the support of a saddle, had to cling desperately to keep from sliding off the back of the horse.

It was only a breathing space. He knew that the instant they were driven off the hard beach and into the softness of the sand beyond, that double weight would stop the gelding abruptly. And when the pursuers overtook them — well, it would probably not be sudden death that they would grant to Speedy.

The girl came suddenly out of her faint with a cry rising from her lips.

The savage voice of Speedy crackled like gunfire at her ear, saying: "Steady. They're trying to murder Crocker and kidnap you. For heaven's sake, believe me."

She had jerked her head around, and now she saw that lean and handsome face, with set jaw, with blazing eyes, and she knew that she had heard the truth.

The wind had loosened from her shoulders the black *mantilla*, and now the long scarf was blown behind them as Isabella Materro swayed suddenly forward in the saddle and began to ride for her life. Speedy gave her the reins. He had enough to do to keep in his place now, and watch the pursuit, without trying to guide the horse, also. And she rode like a master. By the white of her skin, there was good old Castilian blood in her, but there seemed to be a dash of Indian, also, from the way she rode, bending low to cut the wind.

They actually gained a little as they reached the end of the lagoon, but Speedy knew what they must do. Headlong flight could not save them, but, the trees of the marsh arose like a dingy fog above the sands, and toward it he told the girl to ride.

He gave her quick instructions.

"Head straight into the woods. Then slant to the side and stop the horse. Throw hard back on the reins to stop him. And then get off the saddle and do what I do. If I run, run with me. If I drop for the ground, drop beside with me."

"I hear," said the girl. The voice blew back over her shoulder to Speedy. "And Lew . . . he's been hurt?"

"He's nicked. He's not broken," said Speedy. "Now. Now!"

He beat the racing horse with the flat of his hand to drive it across the narrow stretch of open beech toward the trees. There in the cover, if only he could pick the right place, was Crocker and Crocker's steady gun. But no — Crocker had said that he was no good with weapons. Whatever happened, the manhunt must be turned away from Crocker.

A yell of triumph, a long-drawn wolf howl of delight, came bursting out of the throats of the men of San Gallo, when they saw the prey heading in toward the cover. Then the low branches of the trees reached like hands and arms toward Speedy and the girl.

"Stop!" called Speedy, and the darkness shut over them.

The girl obeyed her instructions to the letter. She jerked hard back on the reins. The cow pony came to a halt with braced legs, hurling a big spray of sand before it. And Isabella Materro was already out of the saddle and on the ground.

Speedy, as the horse stopped, had been slung sidewise from his place. He crashed into a bush, scrambled out on hands and knees, and fired straight out from among the trees toward the beach. He could see nothing, but he could hear the yelling voices.

Those yells, and the hoof beats, split from directly in front of him and spread off to either side. They had not cared to push home their charge against a man in safe hiding.

Speedy got to his feet. The girl arose. She had done exactly as he commanded, and had thrown herself down beside him. Now she was on her feet, silent, waiting for orders. Shadow covered Speedy, but mottled moonlight played over her. He saw the flashing of her eyes. She was like a deer, as slenderly made and as beautiful.

The heart of Speedy leaped in him savagely. For one moment, he forgot Lew Crocker, who lay somewhere in those woods with a soul on fire.

And then the passion went out of him. For he saw that she was surrounded by fear. Fear of the yelling, shouting, shooting devils who had begun to search the woods — fear of this strange land — fear of the black marsh water that was close to them — fear even of this man who declared that he was trying to rescue her.

He said to her gently: "Crocker was shot through the leg. Not a bad wound. No bone broken. They wanted to keep him until they'd bled him of all his money."

She put her hands against her throat and watched his face with agony in her own.

"They want to murder him. They have orders to do that. From Mateo Materro. But they're going" — he talked straight on, in spite of her faint stifled outcry — "they're going to double-cross Materro. He simply wants you stopped and taken back home, with Crocker put out of the way, but they want to keep you for as much ransom as they can squeeze out of Materro. They tackled Crocker tonight. The ship came in sight in time to keep them from finishing their job. I managed to get him away into the woods. He's out here now, off there to the left. His wound is bandaged up, well enough. That's the story. Our job is to try to find him now. To try to find him before Tim Lynch and the rest come across him and stamp him out."

"We'll find him," said Isabella Materro quietly. "I know we'll find him. Heaven won't let such a man as you fail. And you haven't told me why you do these things. You haven't told me who you are."

"I'm the odd chance," said Speedy. A grin twisted his mouth wry. "I'm the odd chance that might win, after all. But it's just an odd chance . . . just the thing that happens by accident."

"The odd chance?" she repeated slowly. "I don't understand."

"Neither do I exactly," said Speedy. "But all you need to know about me is that I just happened to stumble into the picture. That's why I call myself the odd chance."

She smiled at him. He raised a hand. And out of the near distance, she heard a stealthy sound coming gradually toward them.

Speedy turned toward that noise. Over his face came an expression of animal savagery and pleasure. His body shrank closer to the ground. He began to stalk without a sound toward that approaching whisper of sound.

The girl wavered, then gripped his arm.

"I can't stand it," she whispered.

He turned his head slowly toward her and regarded her with unseeing eyes, for an instant, so intent was he on his work. Then, straightening with a faint sigh, he nodded to her, and drew noiselessly back with her into the shadows among the trees.

# CHAPTER
# TWELVE

By the noise they had heard, it was reasonably clear that they had been spotted and observed by one of the San Gallo men. More than one could hardly have moved with such secrecy, passing like a quiet breeze through the shrubbery.

It seemed what any one of several of that group would do — go keenly on to make the kill for himself, instead of trying to call in nearby friends to assist. There was Tim Lynch, for instance, with enough of resolution in his brutal nature; there was Chive, even more dangerous on any ground except that of sheer strength; Chesty, too, would prove a poisonous enemy. Only the cook and Sailor Joe were apt to be a little heavy and clumsy in the attack. It must be, thought Speedy, some one of the first three that now slipped so quietly through the woods.

Anger worked on the whole body of Speedy just like the grip of a hand.

"Go on, straight on," he commanded. "Go quietly . . . feel your way along from one bit of moonlight to the next. I'm dropping behind for a moment and . . ."

She gripped his arm and clung to him.

"You're going back to kill him as if he were a beast," she said.

"That's what he is," said Speedy. "They're a set of murderers, and I could kill them all."

"I know you could," said the girl. "But if there's bloodshed on account of me, my life is ruined, señor. I shall give up the world and enter a convent if I am the source of murder."

The sincerity of her emotion flowed toward him out of her whole body, her voice, her gesture.

Speedy answered her with a loud groan: "Very well. I'll go back . . . and simply take him off the trail. I won't do what ought to be done to him."

"Don't go back," she pleaded, whispering. "Please don't go back. Let's try to go faster. I can run . . . you'll see if you try me. But don't go back."

"Hush," said Speedy. "I've got to go. It's the only way. Walk straight on, feeling your way."

He dropped away from her, as he spoke, and watched her go slowly on through the dapplings of moonlight. Her head was bowed, her face covered by one hand, and with the other hand she felt the way before her.

Speedy, shrinking a little back from the way they had been following, sank into a small covert of thick shrubs. Something whispered through them, almost from under his knee — a snake, no doubt, and deadly strikes they had in the marshes.

Now, with his straining ears, he heard once more an incredibly slight sound approaching. One could not imagine human feet so light that they would make so little noise among the dead twigs and leaves that covered the ground. Far more clearly he could hear the retreat of the girl.

He tensed himself in readiness, and then relaxed, for he knew that nerve-hardened muscles cannot react with speed. This was not a case for gun work. He knew that, too, because he had promised the girl that there would be no blood.

Well, there was in his hands a magic that he had used many a time before, and he could use it again.

The noise drew closer. A clammy coldness passed over him, as though a wind had breathed on his back. He wanted to look behind him. Danger seemed to be pouring on him, pressing on him through the silence on all sides. Then, in a patch of deep shadow, he was aware of great, glowing eyes, close to the ground, and a moment later a stalking jaguar glided into the next patch of moonlight.

No wonder that footfall had been lighter than human. The beautiful spotted monster stalked on with head down. Speedy saw the play of the immense muscles that draped the shoulders and the forelegs. He saw the great paws laid down with tenderest care. He saw the tail swerving like a snake.

There are tales enough of man-hunting jaguars. Horror jerked Speedy to his feet with a gasp. That lightning hand of his fumbled at the gun, failing to bring it out, for an instant, and in that instant the hunting beast, with a snarl, bounded out of sight — and straight down the path that the girl had followed.

Speedy himself followed, running hard, a blur of terror before his eyes. The girl screamed on a note that shot up into the brain of Speedy.

And now he saw her body lying half supported by the base of a tree trunk. One blow of the jaguar's forepaw could have torn her life out.

He leaned over her. He snatched her up in his arms and carried her into a bright patch of moonlight. There was no sign of a wound. She breathed; she lived.

His groan of relief came shuddering out of his throat as her eyes opened. Now she stood gasping, her hands clutching his arms to steady her swaying body.

"Was it true . . . or a nightmare?" she breathed. "Did I see a monster leaping at me . . . and shooting by me like a great spotted shadow?"

"You saw a jaguar," said Speedy. "That was the thing that ran by you. Thank heaven that it didn't stop for the tenth part of a second. You're not hurt? The beast didn't touch you?"

"No," she said. "I'm not hurt. But there doesn't seem to be . . . any breath in my body."

Yet she was breathing more easily in a moment.

"When you're ready," said Speedy, "we ought to start moving . . . and start moving fast. Those fellows have heard you cry out . . . and they're a lot more dangerous than jaguars."

"Have I ruined everything?" she pleaded. "I can walk now. I'm all right again. I'm sorry that I screamed. There's still an echo of that screech traveling around my brain. But I won't do it again. Trust me not to do it again."

"I'll trust you," said Speedy. "Come on."

He steadied her for a few moments, but then she went on as well as before, stepping cautiously but rapidly behind him, putting her feet down exactly where his had fallen.

More sounds came toward them, the indubitable noise of walking men. Speedy drew the girl back behind a big tree, and waited, while those footfalls came stealthily on.

Then, while the men were still unseen, the voice of Sailor Joe said: "It ain't this way. That yell bore kind of more to the left from here."

"Maybe," said the voice of Chesty.

They came out into the moonlight. Somewhere they had floundered into the bog and now they were drenched almost to the hips, and their clothes were clotted with mud or with slime. They paused, now, to take a breathing spell.

"A mean business," said Chesty, spitting on the ground. "There was snakes back there in that water. There was water moccasins. I seen one of 'em. It give me the chills and fever, too, when I seen the mouth of it open up like a trap."

"Leave that be," answered Sailor Joe. "I don't wanna think about it. There's enough ahead of us without thinkin' about snakes. There's Speedy . . . and that's snakes enough to suit me."

"I wanna get my hands on him," said Chesty. "All I wanna do is to get my hands on him. He's spoiled the whole show . . . and what does he get out of it?"

"Not a bean, as far as I can see," said Sailor Joe. "It ain't nothing but meanness that's brought him into the job. Nothin' but meanness, whatever. And may he be damned for it. Maybe he wants the girl, though?"

"Yeah, maybe it's the girl."

"She's a good looker, and she's what he likely wants," argued Sailor Joe. "But can he get her? It's Crocker that she come to see."

"Yeah, but she ain't a fool," said Chesty. "She's got a brain in her head, and a pair of eyes, too. If she was blind as a bat, she could see a difference between a big honest boob like Crocker, and the champeen wildcat of the world . . . Speedy."

"He's no wildcat . . . he's a hellcat," said Sailor Joe. "He'll walk off with the girl, all right."

"Sure he will. There ain't nobody that does something for nothing," agreed Chesty. "Let's hunt down this way."

They moved off, and were instantly lost among the shadows.

Speedy went on with the girl. He hardly dared to look at her, after what they had overheard, but he felt her eyes on him, presently, as they came to a moonlit stretch. And turning a little, he saw her smiling straight back into his eyes with a perfect confidence and faith.

"People like that could never understand," she said. "But I understand how there can be people like you in the world, who do something for nothing."

There was no doubt in her; there was no fear in her. And once more the heart of Speedy leaped like a bright flame. He had to center his mind firmly on the need of

Lew Crocker in order to banish the temptation and put it firmly away from his mind.

Now they stole through soggy ground, their feet making sucking noises as they walked. They veered away from that spot, and the foul breath of the marsh. Sheering off to the left, Speedy presently knew that he was near the spot where he had left poor Crocker. He had come back in that direction as quickly as he could, but would not Tim Lynch and his men have long preceded him in reaching the place?

That was why the suspense grew heavily in the soul of Speedy as he went on with his companion, and every moment, to right and left, vast, bearded, unhuman faces seemed to be looking out upon them from the trees. That was the effect of the drapings of Spanish moss.

Now and again, while they walked stealthily on, they heard noises of living things *plumping* into the slimy waters of the marsh. Nothing could have been more desolate; the most naked desert under a burning sun would have been a paradise, compared with this haunted wood.

"Now, very carefully," said Speedy. "We're almost where I left Crocker. He may still be there . . . and with Lynch and a few others around the spot, using Crocker for a bait to draw us into the trap. Go like a shadow now."

Like two shadows they went on together, in fact, and so edged through the trees and the shrubs until they were close to the little clearing that Speedy remembered.

He walked first, here; the girl moved just behind him. And so her way was blocked when he came to a sudden halt.

Carefully parting the branches before his face, he could look out into the clearing. The moon had moved in the sky, and now it covered the whole of the bed of moss that had been made for Crocker. But Crocker was no longer stretched upon it; the whole clearing was empty of sight or of sound.

# CHAPTER
# THIRTEEN

Speedy walked on into the clearing. It might be that some of the men of Tim Lynch were waiting for this very thing to happen, but time pressed, and chances had to be taken.

And no voice or gun hailed him.

He reached the bed of thick moss. The imprint of the body of the wounded man was still upon it. And from beside it, Speedy saw at once a trail where he had dragged himself away into the brush.

Speedy beckoned to the girl, then he followed that trail, losing it often, but recovering it in spots of moonlight again. Finally he heard a stirring in the bushes not far before him.

"Crocker," he called cautiously.

The voice of Crocker answered instantly: "Speedy . . . thank heaven you've come back. And Isabella . . . what . . . ?"

She was up and past Speedy like a running deer. When he came to the place, he found Crocker braced against the trunk of a tree, and the girl on her knees beside him.

All the pain of labor and of danger passed instantly out of the mind of Speedy, for he knew that the thing he had done had been worth it all.

He turned his back, and stood for a moment staring off through the trees, making his ears deaf to the joy of that greeting, and smiling a little. It made him feel old and a little world-weary to be so near and yet so far apart from all of this happiness.

But it did not last long. He heard the girl calling to him, and he turned to find their faces lighted more by happiness than by the moon.

"She's told me, Speedy," said Crocker. "No other man in the world would have dared to do what you've done . . . nobody else would have dared to try. And if I can live through the pinch, you're going to find out how I appreciate it. But what's the plan now? Are we just to stay here till help comes from town?"

"We've got to find a better place than this," said Speedy. "Lynch is no fool. Why he hasn't come here . . . with Chesty to guide him . . . I can't imagine. But, after all, you don't matter so much to him. It's Isabella Materro that he wants to have in his hands. Now we'll go ahead if we can find a place where we can lie snug and fight them off even if they spot us. Can you wait here, till I try to spot a place?"

"We'll stay here," said Crocker. "Whatever you do will be the right thing, Speedy."

The girl held up her hand. "Listen," she said.

They were mute, straining their ears, and presently they heard a far-off sound of *crackling*, as though men were walking through the brush. But that *crackling* was joined, almost at once, to a dim roaring noise.

"Fire," said the girl.

"Fire," whispered Crocker.

The three stared at one another.

"They're trying to drive us out into the open," said Speedy gloomily. "And I don't know what we can do about it."

"We've got to go," said Crocker. "What devil put the idea in their minds? They'll burn these dead woods for twenty miles with that fire."

"Is there any open stretch of water?" asked Speedy. "Some place where the fire can't jump the stretch? Or are there any rocks where we'd have shelter from the fire?"

"There's a big stretch of water, a good mile from here. We'd never get to it," said Crocker. "Look. The fire's galloping like a horse."

He pointed up above the tops of the trees, but there was no need to point, for now as the dead wood of that ancient forest and its dry clotting of sunburned moss kindled, showers of sparks flew upward, and immense volumes of smoke, and arms of red flame that made the moonlit sky seem pale. Waves of firelight began to strike through the trees, and throw wavering, terrible shadows.

"We'll do something," said Speedy. "Is there no safe place in the whole marsh? Do you know the lay of the land, Crocker?"

"I know," said Crocker. "There's a freak of a hill of rocks, a quarter of a mile from here. It's generally surrounded with a narrow belt of water. If we could get to that, perhaps the rocks would keep us from being burned. But it's too slim a chance. We've got to give up, Speedy, because . . ."

"Take his legs," Speedy said abruptly to the girl. "I'll manage most of his weight. Try to keep step with me, and the pull of his weight won't hurt his leg so much. Are you ready to take the chance, and fight it through, or do you want to surrender yourself to those thugs out there?"

"I'll fight it through," said the girl.

"D'you hear me, Isabella?" said poor Crocker. "It's a matter of your life, my dear. Go out to the open, both of you. I'll crawl after you . . . it's not far to the edge of the beach. They'll make a bargain with you for your life, Speedy, if they know that they're to have her . . ."

"They'll make no bargains with me," insisted Speedy calmly. "We're all in one boat here. And we'll fight it through together. Are you ready?" he demanded suddenly of the girl.

"Ready," she said.

So they lifted Crocker. He still protested, but the two marched on, until he had to set his teeth hard, because groans were forcing through his lips among his words of appeal to Isabella to fly for her life.

Behind them came the red wall of the fire. Huge tufts of flaming moss sailed up on the arms of the conflagration, and a wind arose, drawn inward from all sides by the strength of the upward draft of the heat.

From a clearing, they saw the hill that Crocker had mentioned, and the heart of Speedy sank at the sight of it, for it was low — very low. And although it was like a heap of broken rock, yet it was overgrown with a tangle of vines, it seemed.

However, they would try it. The waves of flame might sweep over that rock and sear away their flesh, but on the other hand they might make a wall of loose stone against the fire. It was a chance, and a lean one. But when Speedy looked back into the face of the girl, he saw her grim with resolution.

What could one wish to find in a woman more than was in her?

They hurried on. The forest fell away on either side of them. Before them lay a narrow belt of water, not many yards across, and beyond that was the hill of stones.

Speedy, stepping in, found himself up to the knees in slime. The loose mud of the bottom sucked at his feet. Every step was more and more difficult, until suddenly his forward foot sank several inches. When he tried to draw it up, he failed. A powerful suction was working on his leg. Two strong efforts merely sank his whole body to the hips.

And then he understood.

That wild and indomitable heart of his which had faced so many dangers, and triumphed joyously in overcoming them, now quailed. Better to face the fire itself, helplessly. Better to die in any conceivable way than by the horror that now had hold on him — for the deep quicksand of the marsh had fast hold on his feet and was drawing him down.

# CHAPTER
# FOURTEEN

"Isabella can you step? Are you deep in the mud?" Speedy asked, holding himself as still as possible.

"I can move my feet . . . but the mud is trying to hold them," said the girl, panting.

"Back up toward the shore, then," said Speedy. "Back up toward the dry land. Pull Crocker back with you. Crocker, turn over . . . face down . . . and walk yourself back on your hands. I'm caught in the quicksand."

Neither of the others cried out when they heard it. They did merely as they were told. And as Crocker was moved back to a little distance, his body supported on his hands, his legs held by the girl, he lifted one arm above the water and stretched it toward Speedy.

"Throw yourself on your back and give me your hand," said Crocker.

Speedy did as he was told. The foul, slimy water covered him. He caught the hand of Crocker, and received a strong pull. But the quicksand held his feet with a terrible power. Only little by little did the sleek mud give up its grasp. The strength of the pull caused his body to sink under the surface. He closed his eyes against the foulness that poured over his face. He held his breath to strangulation, while, little by little, the fatal grasp of the quicksand relinquished its hold.

Suddenly he was free. He rose to hands and knees, gasping, sputtering out the mud and the rotten slime of the marsh.

A moment later, he was on his feet, helping Crocker back toward the dry, firm land.

They were three dripping statues of mud, three writhing, mud-blackened bodies.

Before them, the fire burned yellow and orange and deep-red as it advanced in a wall. Sometimes there were purple streaks and sometimes there were bits of intense blue. Water-soaked logs, closed in the grip of that furnace heat, exploded, casting burning gases high into the air where the sparks, the hands of fire, and above all the flaming tresses of the Spanish moss were already rising and falling.

The roaring of the fire increased, and a vast rushing sound as though of running waters in a deep cañon. The wet marsh *hissed* like a million snakes; the wet tree roots exploded, shaking the earth. And the fierce breath of the fire rolled more and more intensely toward the three.

The whole marsh was lighted, as far as the eye could stretch. Writhing tree trunks appeared like imprisoned creatures, twisted by the agony of fear, but unable to flee from destruction. And across the horrible, green face of the marsh real life was stirring — countless sleek or ugly shapes wriggling through the water.

There was a slightly narrower crossing toward the base of the hill that now seemed a great fortress, a place of security. Silently, carrying his greater share of the weight of Crocker, Speedy took the way to it. He placed Crocker on the ground. There were old logs, half buried in the ground, half rotting into it, dissolving with moisture and decay. He began to tear these up. Sometimes they broke away in sections. And he hurled them out into the water.

The girl understood that idea at once, and lent her aid. She was not strong enough to manage the heavy sections, but she found fallen branches, and carried these out. They dashed the green water into foam, running back and forth, gasping for breath as the heat of the fire made all the air about them like the burning breath from an oven.

Crocker made one appeal.

"Speedy, you can't save me!" he shouted. "I'm done for. Save yourselves, and heaven bless you both!"

They did not pause in their work. They did not even glance at one another, the girl and Speedy. For long ago, the mutual understanding had been silently arrived at between them — the three of them would win or lose together.

A frightful howl came out of the edge of the woods. Then the splendid mottled body of a jaguar hurtled through the air, struck the water near the base of the hill of rocks, and disappeared under the water for an instant. It rose again, the head and the shoulders standing clear, the tail lashing above the surface.

But as it struggled, the quicksand gripped its feet. It sank lower instantly. Another prolonged howl of despair and fear came like the voice of a demon out of that throat, and then the great beast was still, waiting patiently, its head barely above the surface, until the waters should close over it.

"Now!" cried Speedy to the girl, and they sprang to Crocker, and lifted him.

The flames were searing the backs of their heads as they advanced into the water, slipping, staggering. It was a broken, an incomplete line of water-logged branches and tree trunks that they had dropped into the marsh, where the wood in nearly every case sank slowly to the bottom. They had to feel with their feet for that precarious bridge. Slowly they went across. A dozen times their feet slipped off into the treacherous ooze of the bottom. But in every case they found a firm grip for the other foot, and saved themselves.

They were more than halfway across when Crocker turned suddenly into a limp weight, twice as hard to handle as he had been before. The terrible heat, the excitement, the fear, and above all the long agony that he endured from his wound had caused him to faint, and Speedy, with dread in his heart, wondered if they were to fail, after all.

But they went floundering on until they passed the last of the wooden causeway that they had flung into the water. Into the ooze they stepped, but their feet bit through it, and found a sure support in the rocky bottom, where the roots of the hill spread out.

In a moment, they were across. They put Crocker down and turned — reeking, filthy, blackened faces — to stare at one another.

Crocker recovered with a groan. It was hardly heard. The mere matter of his fainting was nothing now. For they had reached to the verge of their meager chance of safety.

But Speedy looked back, and, across the fire-reddened face of the water, he saw merely the muzzle of the jaguar appearing above the slime. The moments were few before the ending of that fierce life.

He stepped back, therefore, fumbled through the foulness of the water, found a half-buried tree trunk, and barely managed to drag it to the surface. He was wasting moments that would be precious to the saving of three human lives, but he could not let the poor dumb beast die without one gesture toward saving it.

He went to the edge of the hill opposite the drowning jaguar, stepped into the water to his knees, and flung the trunk as far toward the mark as he could.

The splash it raised caused the head of the beast to disappear. It was in sight again instantly. The water around it lashed into foam with the madness of its efforts to climb onto this heaven-sent new purchase for its claws. Half its body lifted suddenly clear. It bounded for forward, dashed into the water again, and then floundered safely to the shore.

Speedy already had lifted the body of Crocker. With the girl he was stumbling up the sharp slope of the hill. They rounded it. The rocky shoulders shut away most of the blast of the heat, and they found themselves in a nest of huge stones, a veritable haven that seemed to have been framed for them by Nature itself.

# CHAPTER
# FIFTEEN

They fell to work with frenzied hands, heaving the smaller stones up and raising the wall about them, higher and higher. They had almost closed it at the lower side, when a wet body glided through the aperture and lay cowering on the ground. It was the jaguar again, fear-maddened, fear-subdued.

"It won't harm you!" called Speedy suddenly. For he remembered how the mountain lion flees at the side of the deer, when the forest fire is driving all life before it.

Crocker, who sat gun in hand, held the fire of his revolver.

In fact, to fire with such a weapon at close range might be fatal to all three of them, for even in its death agonies the jaguar might destroy them.

It lay still. As the encircling wall of the fire surrounded the hill, the big brute shuddered, and dropped its head between its paws, and lay with tightly blinked eyes. Its tail twitched, now and again. Otherwise it lay as though dead.

Meantime, those three human lives endured the oven heat that poured through the air. Sparks fell on them. A flaming mass of Spanish moss dropped down inside their enclosure, where Speedy trampled it out, as the jaguar moaned.

The *roaring*, the *crackling*, the explosions of water-logged tree trunks kept up the incredible din. And the three, wiping the slime from their faces, endured, and never spoke. The girl sat beside Crocker, her arms about him, her face on his shoulder.

As the red waves of the firelight played over them, Crocker stared grimly at Speedy, and Speedy stared grimly back. Thirst raged in them. Sweat poured from their bodies. And still they were as silent as the wild beast that had sought shelter with them.

Then, by slow degrees, the torrent of the fire receded. Speedy stood up and looked over the edge of their improvised stone well. On one side, the burned-over marsh presented 1,000 glowing points of light, where logs were still burning; and there were two or three hollow trunks that were burning like enormous candles, and throwing reflections out over the stagnant waters. Overhead, the moon was dead in the sky; the pale gray of the morning had commenced to steal around the horizon. And on the other side, the living wall of the fire rushed on with increasing speed, fanned by the wind of its own raising. Such was the immensity of the heat that the green vines that overgrew the hill of rocks had caught fire. In some places they had entirely burned away. In other places they offered a pattern of glowing veins laid over the stones.

But the wind that followed the fire was making life more endurable. That same wind flung the flames now and again far ahead of the regular march of the conflagration. Here and there a solitary tree caught and seemed to explode upward in a torrent of sparks and shooting fires. And always, out of the air, there was a continual rein of fine ashes, and little bits of charcoal, sometimes still glowing.

That was the picture that Speedy saw, and far off, along the beach, were two riders — small, distant figures. And on the other side of the marsh, three more appeared.

What were the thoughts of the murderers, now they were sure that they had burned their victims? What was the savage rage in the heart of Tim Lynch, when he thought of the wasted ransom money, that fortune that he had made sure of drawing out of the wealth of Mateo Materro? And in far-away Mexico, what would Materro himself think, when he learned that his murder plot had failed, and that his heiress was safe in America with the man she loved?

The girl stood up beside him, and they watched the sun rise. The air cooled. The frightful breath of the fire was far removed.

"If our man lived to ride through and get help . . . ," said Speedy, thinking half aloud. "If the help comes before Lynch and the rest know that we're here and try to rush the hill and take us . . ."

"They'll never try," said the girl. "Their spirits are broken. They've failed too often against you and they'll never dare to stand up to you now. Not if there were fifty of them against you."

There was no weariness in the eye of Speedy as he looked down at her. But he merely said: "Tell me about

Mateo Materro . . . that uncle of yours. What sort of a fellow is he?"

"Gentle to his friends, and terrible to his enemies," she said. "A tall, old man, with a beautiful, stern face. He has been like a father and a mother to me. No matter what he has done, I never could stop loving him. But . . . he hates all Americans. To see me married to an American would be worse to him than to see me dead. Oh, ten thousand times worse. To save me from that, he would have had not one man killed, but a hundred of them, and he would have felt that his hands were clean after the killings."

"And now that you're here?" said Speedy.

"I'm the last of his blood," said the girl gently. "For a year, he'll harden his heart . . . perhaps only for a month. And after that . . . well, after that it will be in all things as my husband wishes it to be."

The jaguar rose, and slunk sullenly out of the enclosure — then bolted down the slope at full speed, maddened by the ancient fear of man.

The sun climbed higher. Speedy, continually spying over the landscape, saw the distant riders draw to a focus at the ranch house, and disappear inside of it.

They had given up, then, and believed their victims to be dead. And now, if poor, wounded Danny had managed to break through for help? Well, even if that were not the case, Lynch and his men had lost their battle at every point.

Crocker, exhausted by the terrible night, lay on his back, sleeping heavily.

The sun climbed toward the zenith, filling the little enclosure with heat almost like that of the fire during the night. And then, far away across the plains, a dust cloud rolled up, grew in height and clearness, and gradually dissolved into the forms of many riders. Danny had broken through, after all.

Yet still there was no sudden outpouring of men from the ranch house. They would not believe, perhaps, that the rescuing party could have come so fast. They would not leave the whiskey jug, either, beyond all doubt, unless they had given themselves plenty of consolation for that night of complicated disappointments.

Nearer and nearer the cavalcade came, a score — no, thirty men — sweeping along. And at last the men in the ranch house were warned. They came pouring out, guns in their hands. They mounted, fighting. One of them fell. Some of the posse had dismounted and lay on the ground, to give accuracy to their fire. Others charged straight in. The thing was over in a moment. The surrender was complete before the sounds of the distant firing had ceased to float through the air to the watchers.

For that wedding, the entire town turned out. Everyone of importance within fifty miles found an excuse for coming in, and the church was crowded. The hour for the ceremony arrived. Still the bridegroom tapped on the floor the crutches that would help him to the altar, and shook his head.

"We can't be married without the best man. We can't be married without Speedy."

Isabella Materro shook her head, also, and made a beautiful gesture to indicate the utter impossibility of the ceremony unless Speedy were there.

It was an hour after the appointed time, before a ragged little boy managed to get into the church and at last into the room where the couple waited, carrying a note in his hand.

Crocker tore it open impatiently, and scanned the contents twice over. Then he passed it to the girl. She read:

Dear Old Man:

I thought I could go through with it. But, at the last minute, my heart weakened. For one thing, there are a great many reasons why I never like to show myself as I really am to any crowd. It would be dangerous for a good many reasons, some of which you know. For another thing, if I am a witness at your marriage, my real name must go down in the book, and that name is a secret that I never can let the world know. So I can only wish you and Isabella the happiest lives, and sign myself your affectionate friend,

Speedy

# A WATCH AND THE WILDERNESS

Frederick Faust began seeking other markets for his fiction when, beginning in 1933, Street & Smith began lowering his rate of 5¢ a word first to 4¢, and then 3¢. Among others, his stories began to appear in *Argosy*, *Adventure*, and *Collier's*. Three stories were published in *Elk's Magazine*. The first, "Paradise", appeared in May, 1935, followed by "Virginia Creeper" in August, 1937. "A Watch in the Wilderness" appeared in the September, 1940 issue, one of four short stories published that year; his writing output having dramatically decreased by then. It is a poignant Civil War story dealing with a brief encounter between a Texas Rebel and a Connecticut Yankee.

Sometimes a thing gets stuck in your mind like a burr in a dog's hair and it won't come out without tearing. It might be the whine of a windmill that needs oiling, or the *click-clunk* of railroad wheels over the rail ends, or mostly it will be a tune you can't shake out of your ears, but what stayed with me longest was something a Yank said back when I was one of Marse Robert's boys.

All those days the noise of the guns never ended, the cannon hurting our ears and the musketry *crackling* like burning stubble. Sometimes the rain dropped like night falling; sometimes it blew away like dust before it touched the ground; sometimes it came sheeting straight down from tubs and buckets, you might say, wetter than all the Mondays in the world. The woods stood close around us like a permanent fog, with the shells cutting lanes and avenues into it, but never punching all the way through to clean, open sky. It was all mud and mist; there was not hope or sense in anything except that we knew Marse Robert was not far away, thinking and thinking.

That day a damn' Yank climbed somewhere into the trees above our trenches and began to shoot us one by one, taking his time and spotting the best men as though he came from Texas himself and knew us by name. What with the uproar and the crowding of the trees and the rain and the powder smoke blowing, we couldn't locate him. Sometimes we thought we heard the *clang* of his rifle, thin and high over the battle, like the sound of a silver spoon falling in a room filled with people and noise, but wherever we looked there was only the fog of the trees and mist in the air.

He shot John Tucker between the neck and the shoulder, so that his head fell over on one side. My friend Tad Crothers and Loomis carried him back from the line, and I was best pleased to see Tad out of there. He shot Phil Lawrence through the back. Phil had been singing a song to keep us warm and his mouth went on making the words and smiling for a moment. Bernard and Kendricks carried him back. And then, by God, he shot Tommy Dean spang through the forehead, so there was no need to carry Tom back at all.

We tried to heap up the embankment of our trench to save us from the rifle but there wasn't a single trenching tool. We had to knife out the mud with our bayonets and ladle it up, but it turned to yellow soup and went sluicing away.

We had marched all the way from Manassas to Gaines's Mill to Freyzer's Farm and the second Manassas, where Marse Robert fooled them so bad, and on to Antietam's trouble, and Fredericksburg that was so easy, and Chancellorsville where we stretched legs so long, and Gettysburg, full of mighty bad luck, and now we were whopping Butcher Grant in the wilderness. But it seemed as though we had done these things for Marse Robert only to have one Yank let the blood out of all of us and turn our trench into a damned red latrine. We were so scared that we wouldn't look at one another. All our dead came crowding up so close in my thoughts that I wouldn't turn my head right and I wouldn't turn it left, I felt them so near. Then Billy Wendell gave the yell. There wasn't an officer in sight so we had only the yell to lead us as we slopped out of our hole in the ground and went screeching through the woods. We followed the little paths and blind lanes that the cannon had cut open for us, but we couldn't find anything in the trees so after a while we turned and went back.

When we returned, I was behind the others because the mud was bogging me down. I saw Red Stuart shot through the back as he got to the edge of the trench. By the way of him falling and throwing out his arms I knew that he'd dropped out of my sight and out of my life and all that was left of that partner was no more than a rag doll that lay face down in the slime. I didn't try to get back to the trench then. I got down behind a bush and huddled there like when I was a boy in the attic bed, listening to the winter outside the house. Times like that I used to want to be near Pa, and now I wanted Marse Robert — as though he didn't have more things than just Texans to think about. Pretty soon I heard the trenches howl like a hound dog that's had a ramrod cut into his back, then all the rifles went off *crash*, so I knew the Yank had taken another man. I was glad that I couldn't tell whose dying it was that had hurt all the boys so much, but a lump came up in my throat that I swallowed and swallowed and swallowed, while I looked around me into the trees, high up where the Yank somewhere sat like God in a cloud making thunder, making lightning, except that this lightning couldn't be seen.

There was a bird on the tip of a branch, singing. It was the month of May and in spite of the rain and in spite of the battle, the spring of the year that was locked up in him so long was bursting out. I couldn't hear him whistle, but by the beating of his wings and the ruffling of his throat feathers I could see his song. Not ten feet from him, a cannon ball clipped a branch out of the side of a big tree, but the crashing down of that bough was no more to him than the fall of a feather from his nest. He was no more afraid of battle than Marse Robert. I kept looking at him until I saw something queer about the forking of that tree where the branch had been shot away. The queerness was in the stub of a broken branch. The shape of it seemed wrong. I couldn't tell why until it came home to me quick and hard, like a slap on the mouth. It wasn't any branch at all. It was the boot on a man's foot and part of his shank. That was all I had for a target but one of Marse Robert's boys didn't ask for more than a fingerhold to pull a damn' Yank out of a tree. I got the old musket up and steadied her until she laid her hold right on the thin of the shank. It didn't seem to amount to enough. I guessed where the rest of him might be and aimed at the heart of my guess. Then I squeezed the trigger.

The foot jumped out of sight almost like I had shot it off. I laid back small behind my bush and sang "Little

**118**

Brown Jug", though I couldn't hear myself. I sang, because I knew I had him. A Texas boy you can punch full of bullets, but a Texas life won't run out through little holes like that. Only the life of a Yank is like a bubble, and, if you prick it anywhere, it busts and it's gone away. I kept looking for him to loosen his hold and come down, bumping his way from branch to branch. But he didn't come. There was a runnel of water that came from the foot of that tree toward the bush where I lay and after a while the water in it began to turn red, so that I knew his blood was soaking along the bark of the tree to the ground. You couldn't have told, by the red of it, who was dying, Confederate or Yank. I kept watching the place in the tree and seeing the bird that sang beside it until finally a musket dropped. It *whammed* against the lower branches, bouncing from one to the other until it landed in the pine needles. Still the Yank didn't follow his gun.

After a while I got up.

"Hey, Yank," I said, "come on down and let's have a little talk."

I laughed when I said it and hurt my belly, because I hadn't eaten for so long. I pressed my hand over the pain until it was easier and kept looking up through the leaves, but he didn't come down. I glanced over to the trench and there were all the boys waving me in. A Yank shell came along and took the upper half of Tim Maynard away with it but nobody ducked back into the trench. It seemed that other kinds of death didn't matter except what came out of the rifle of the Yank in the tree.

Then he came down. His legs were crazy. They seemed already dead below the hips but he helped himself slowly from place to place. I enjoyed seeing the Yank come down to surrender and I enjoyed seeing how the one side of the tree was red with his blood, but I could feel an ache in my own side when I saw where the blood was running from his body. When he got to the lowest branch, I held up my hands and helped him the rest of the way, though that hurt my stomach again. Finally he was lying on the ground. The boys in the trench had seen and they gave me a yell.

I stood and looked at my Yank. He wasn't much older than my nineteen and there wasn't much to him. He didn't have the look of strength in his neck. There was no Texas rawhide in him. On the ground he wouldn't have been worth a hang, though he had done pretty good up a tree.

I sat down on a stump and looked at him, and then down the corduroy road that ran off among the trees through the mud. So much artillery had traveled across it that the logs were splintered and warped in the center and their ends stuck up. Some of them were pounded as soft as cloth where the wheels had bumped them. The ends of them dripped mud. It was queer, sitting there in the rain and knowing that we didn't need Marse Robert any more just then.

I got a twist of grass and mopped the sweat away from the Yank's face. When a man begins to leak blood he is always thirsty, so I offered him my canteen but his hand couldn't hold it. I steadied it for him and he drank. Afterward his head lay back and he looked at me. Then he closed his eyes and seemed dead.

He had on good-looking boots as soft as glove-leather, so I pulled off one of them and threw away my own shoe. His boot fitted me fine. It came onto my foot as smooth as silk. I felt sort of grateful. If his boots were so good maybe the rest of him was just as fine, so I opened up his coat and had to let out a holler, for the whole inside of that coat was lined with chamois as soft as the breast of a duck. Why should he care if Marse Robert's boys were stuck in the rain and the mud when he could keep himself as dry and warm as a muffin?

Besides the coat there was a flannel shirt as soft as down and beneath that was an undershirt as sure enough linen as one of General Hood's handkerchiefs. I rubbed it between my fingers and laughed to myself, thinking how fine I'd be from the skin out. Before I pulled off his clothes there were the pockets to go through, so I sat down cross-legged with the whole grab bag all to myself. I found three handkerchiefs, two as clean as a cat's whiskers; a pocket knife with blades of razor steel; a sewing kit in a flat pig-skin case with a scissors in it so neat it made me laugh; a pocket-size book in a language I couldn't read; a chunk of good hog-sausage wrapped in paper — I started eating the sausage; a purse with $3.15 in real gold pieces — one for me, one for my friend Tad, and one to send home to Judy Anne. It was like picking things off a Christmas tree — there was always something more to find. Shoved down into a special trouser pocket there were

**121**

two razors of good Sheffield steel, and, when I saw all that heap of loot I knew there was enough to make camp talk for a month. That was before I got at the watch in its own leather-lined pocket inside the coat. When that was in my hand, I stopped thinking of everything else and just damned the whole world, specially the Yankee part of it.

There isn't much that a man can need and love and always keep with him. Even a wife stays at home. Only a man's horse and dog go with him and a straight-shooting gun, and a watch that keeps time.

This was a regular jim-dandy, the kind you put under your pillow and press in the dark of night and it chimes back the hour as true as the church bells of a Sunday morning. They don't make a watch like that; they build it. And the builders are all Swiss with eyes finer than needle points that could unravel a spider web into strands like it was a rope. When they get through, you have a watch that will keep time whether you're shooting wild geese, or riding herd, or just sitting on the front porch watching the world turn itself over on its back. If you feel weary of waiting for things to happen, you open up the watch, the big outside cover and the thin inside cover that never stops shining, and you see the wheels going jog-jog back and forth, all at a balance, all together, under and over, side by side, married together, never to part, and in the noise of every tick there is a little golden, chiming sound that says: "Good news . . . good news!"

Well, just to one side of the middle of that watch my bullet had gone through and spread the insides clean through the Yank. I shook it in my hand, and I hated the damned Yanks, and I hated the damned war, and I knew what death was. Anyway, I opened up the case and inside the big front cover there was something that stirred the hair of my head like murder right under my eyes. For somebody, working small, had painted the picture of a girl on the gold, and my bullet had taken off the bigger half of her head. There was only left some of her hair and a part of her smile, and, by the jumping, it might have been Judy Anne! I mean she was so young that, like Judy Anne, she was a little bit scrawny in the throat and in the arms, but what was left of her smile showed me the whole of her just as I could see Judy Anne whirling at a dance, or riding a horse, or just sitting still.

Just about that time I thought I heard a bird singing and it seemed to me that I must be crazy; but I wasn't, for a quiet time had come in the battle the way it always does, as though even war had to have a catnap for a minute or two, and in the pause I was hearing that bird just busting himself on the tip of the branch. Right then the Yank, that I had thought was dead, began to speak. I snapped shut the watch, quick, and moved to cover up the pile of loot. I was scared as though he had a gun pointed. But he wasn't even looking at me. He was staring up at the bird and saying words that I didn't understand. The sound of them was *"Carmina morte carent."* He stopped talking but he seemed to keep on smiling, so it was a minute after the battle had started roaring again before I realized that he was dead for sure. I put the watch back in its pocket and went home through the rain to our trench.

What the Yank had said kept ding-donging in my mind and the look of him smiling, like my brother Pete lazing in bed on a Sunday morning. I wondered what the words meant, but even if the Yank had talked English I wouldn't have understood. We could have met twenty times and even drank together and still I would have hated his Connecticut and he would have despised my Texas. He'd been raised mighty careful and cultivated by hand like a truck garden, while I'd been turned loose on a horse; so the only way I could introduce myself was with a bullet, and so he was lost the minute he was found. I got to thinking of Judy Anne so hard that I was homesick. All I wanted was to see her or know the meaning of what the Yank had said.

The boys crowded around me and started making a fuss. They seemed gladder to have me back, almost, than I was to be there.

Tad Crothers said: "Hey, didn't he have two boots?"

I reached down and pulled off the Yankee's boot. It was kind of familiar, feeling the mud go squash around my bare toes; it was kind of a comfort. Behind me, I could feel the rain soaking into the blades of the pocket knife, and into the pig-skin sewing kit to get at the needles and the scissors that would just have fitted the fingers of Judy Anne and I could feel the fine teeth of rust beginning to eat the edges off the steel. Then along came Lieutenant Carrington, chewing something.

I said: "Give me a chew of that tobacco, Lieutenant."

124

He spat out a chunk of slippery bark and said: "I wish it were."

"Lieutenant," I said, "what's the meaning of this . . . 'Carmina morte carent?'"

He said: "Where did you go to school?"

I said: "That's the trouble. I didn't."

A big shell went by with a sound like sailcloth tearing. We both ducked a little. He said, looking after the shell: "It means . . . 'Songs are immune to death.' Where did you hear that?"

"I don't know," I answered him. "But somehow it just got stuck in my head."

I looked over to where the bird had been singing in the tree but it was too far away to be seen, or perhaps it was tired of singing all by itself and had gone off looking for company.

# THE GOOD BADMAN

"The Good Badman" was first published in 1926 in the January 30<sup>th</sup> issue of Street & Smith's *Western Story Magazine*. That year saw eleven short novels and eleven serials published in that magazine; one serial and one short novel appeared in different magazines. "The Good Badman" is a pursuit story told by the protagonist, Ed Garver, who is accused of murder by his longtime football rival from high school. Originally published under Faust's George Owen Baxter byline, this is its first appearance in book form.

# CHAPTER
# ONE

You hear other fellows talk about hard luck, but, believe me, they don't know what they're talking about. They're amateurs. When they hear me, it's the world's professional champion that's talking.

Before I open up on the real story here, I'll give you an idea, first, about how things run for me, right all the way along. You take the way it was in high school.

I don't throw that in about high school to make any hit with you, by flashing a lot of education — because I never had too much. I got by, but it was a squeeze. You know how it is. I was pretty good in geometry until algebra got mixed into the deal; after that everything was pretty much a blank. I got along in English until they started a change of pace and brought on the poetry. I never needed no poetry to earn my Saturday night's pay envelope. Schools are all right for those that like them; I didn't like them.

My old man was set on having me be everything that he wasn't. He was a roughneck and a hard egg. He was so mean that you couldn't speak to him before noon. He couldn't even read a newspaper, and my mother had to hold his hand when he tried to sign his name. He was dreadfully ashamed of not being able to read or to write, but he would have killed anybody that dared to suggest that much to him.

Well, he wanted it fixed so that I would never be ashamed of my ignorance. That was why he sent me to high school, and even aimed at having me go on to college. I got to laugh when I even think of it. The old man didn't have no sense of humor.

He sent me to high school to get an education, and I stayed on there just because I wanted to play football.

You see, when I sat at a desk and stared at the pages of a textbook, the print would blur. I would see, trotting across that page from left to right, not letters but a lobo on the trail; I would see the boys out at a roundup, or somebody bulldogging a yearling.

That was where I belonged. I was born on the range; I grew up on the range. I knew range work, and I knew range ways. I could read the mind of a steer a lot better than I could ever read the mind of a writer. Of course, the old man was wrong to want me to be at any school.

However, when I got interested in football that was different. They thought a lot of football in that high school. They had a track team, too. I couldn't jump high enough or far enough; I couldn't run long enough or fast enough; I couldn't fit into that track team at all.

Football was different. I came into my height and my weight pretty quick. I never weighed more than 150. But, at sixteen, I was pretty close to my full size. I got harder later on, but I never got any meaner. I loved fighting. It was like booze to me. Football, when you get through talking fancy about it, is just a fine fight.

I didn't have the snap, the old coach said, for a back-field man. I didn't have the speed for an end, the steadiness for a center, or the weight for a guard.

On a high-school team I could manage to do in one place, and that was as a tackle. Some can have their other jobs on a football team. Some like to play last defense and run the whole team as quarterback. Some like to be heroes at halfback, running the ends and splitting the line. Others like to be fullback and smash over the line for the touchdowns, and some like to run down under the punts, and flash away to pull down the forward passes. There are those who like to be in the center of the line that won't go down. As for me, I like the tackle's job.

It's a sweet place. Where does the other team try to make its yardage through the line? Through center and guard, it can only make feet. Around the ends is a big gamble, likely to wind up in losses. Forward passes, double passes, and trick formations are all very fine, but risky. There never was a great team, and there never will be one, that wasn't founded on the main essential, which is grinding out the yardage, inside or outside of tackle. When the other quarterback begins howling his signals, you may think what you want about trick plays and all that. The chances are about one in two that, no matter what the other possibilities are, he will shoot his interference and his ball at one of the tackles.

I have got to take this chance to give myself a cheer. I was a sweet tackle. I was a regular bird, believe me — not more than 150 pounds, as I was saying. For high school, that was enough. I could throw myself along the ground with my chest almost touching it, reach up through lifting knees and smashing feet, grab the carrier of the ball from beneath, and feel him falling on his nose.

They hated to send end runs around my side of the line. Many a time I've squeezed through and slammed the bird with the ball. When the tackle breaks through, he throws the runner for a sweet little five- or six-yard loss. They hated my face, I tell you, when they wanted to make a kick. Many a time you would hear the other quarterback sing out: "Smith and Jones and Murphy. Watch that slippery sneak . . . that Garver."

Sure. Garver is my name; I forgot to tell it to you before.

The attack was what I liked the best. The quarterback on my team sure loved me. He would come along, in a pinch, and he would say: "We got to have five yards, kid. Can you open a hole for me?"

Mostly I could. Sometimes I would have to turn myself into a bird and throw myself at the other tackle and the other end, hit the tackle with my head and shoulders and the end with my hips and legs — so that they could shoot the play between tackle and guard. Sometimes I would have to turn in and smear some big stiff of a tackle or a guard when they wanted to shoot the play outside of me. That's about half the game of football in the line — learning to pick yourself up and go throw yourself at something or at somebody.

Of all the swell things in the world, there is nothing to beat the time when you see a gent come tearing down the field, weaving in and out behind his interference and getting up full speed. There is nothing to beat it, when you leave the ground while he's still twenty feet away, dive for him, and jam your shoulder into his legs so dog-goned hard that your whole side turns numb. You feel him sag in the center and then come down with a *whack* that dislocates his digestion, as you might say. No, there is nothing much sweeter than that.

When you take a good, broad look at everything, I got to admit that, as a tackle, I was as good as there was. I tell you what they used to do. They would use up their best linemen on my side of the line, and they used to use them up fast, because, when I threw myself at the other fellow, I knew how to make it hurt. Mostly, too, I had to play my whole side of the line. Our coach never had too much. I would usually have to have a big soft sap of a boob playing guard beside me, and a little featherweight end with pretty legs, playing outside of me. So I was doing three jobs instead of one.

Once I was a hero. That was in my last year, when I was eighteen, and we came to my last big game with Whitman High School that had beat us the year before with a flock of trick plays. I had given my left shoulder a bad wrench the week before, and I had to sit on the bench and watch Whitman make a flock of fools out of our team. They got a touchdown in the first quarter, and they should have scored every other period, except for some fumbles. In the last quarter they began a straight march for our goal, not using any tricks, just straight football.

"This is not a defeat . . . this is a disgrace," said the coach, as he saw our boys staggering and flopping like wet hens. "Garver, for heaven's sake, take a chance and go in there at tackle, will you?"

I could feel that I was gonna be a hero, when I peeled off my blanket and went in. I felt nice and light in the legs, mean in the head, and itchy in the hands, the way that a hero should. The crowd gave me a fine little cheer — I was a last hope — and I felt pretty good.

I said to the Whitman quarterback as I took up my place: "Try me, you sucker, and I'll make a boob out of you and your fancy team."

"The bigger they are, the harder they fall," said this fresh, red-headed kid sarcastically.

That was funny, because I wasn't big — not in pounds. Dog-gone me if he didn't shoot the very first play right at my spot in the line. The tackle and the guard did themselves into a Chinese tangle that I couldn't get through, and there was I, lying on my stomach, and the Whitman halfback walking over me. I got up ten yards closer to our goal.

"Garver," asked my quarter, "are you sick? What happened?"

"Nothing," I answered, taking a handful of mud out of my eye. "You shut up and let me mind my business, kid."

"How do you like that, Garver?" asked the Whitman quarter.

"Fine. Try it again. I was getting warmed up."

Well, sir, he was game, and he *did* try me. I split through that guard and tackle and their Chinese tangle like they were made of cardboard. I dumped the interference, and I drove that big, fine halfback about a yard into the mud. They had to throw a bucket of water into his face before he came to.

"That's a sample!" I called to the red-headed quarterback, whose name was Les Burns. "You come again and get the rest of the pie."

"I'll spread you all over the face of the field before I'm through with you!"

But he didn't shove the next play at me. He sent it around the other end, and, when the tackle was made, Whitman was one measly little half yard from our goal line. The bleachers were busting their throats. I knew that would be too big a temptation for Les Burns. He would want to score that touchdown himself, and he would want to score it through me. Pretty soon, he shot the interference at the other side of our line, but, while the rest of the boys piled in that direction, I wasn't deceived any. I figured that the big play would be Les Burns, piling straight at me, and I was right.

The interference had pulled the rest of our team into that play, and Les had hoped that it would take me in, too. Here he came like a house on fire. When he saw me, he set his teeth and wrinkled his nose and tried to knock me off with a straight left. Ducking under a straight left was the best thing that I did. I didn't wait for him. I went to meet him. I hit Les Burns, and I had to take him on my left shoulder. I hit him so hard that I could hear the bone *crunch*, but I dumped him good and plenty. The wind went out of him like a busted bladder and the football skidded through the mud ahead of me.

The pain in my shoulder was driving me wild. It lifted me onto my feet quicker'n a wink, and I scooped up that ball and started racing down the field as hard as I could run. Every step I took, that broken left arm swung and hung and dangled around in front of me. The bleachers were fairly screaming on one side of the field, and there were thousands of tons of silence on the other. I was sprinting harder than I ever did before, with the white line jumping behind me quicker than you could count. I heard them pounding on behind me. Hearing them breathing, I dodged to the side. The big fullback dived straight past me and made a furrow in the mud. There were others coming. A hard tackle hit me, and I heard the voice of Les Burns cursing me in a sort of a whine as he brought me down.

The speed we were traveling at turned me over and brought me to my feet again. A couple of them were trying to hold me, but I managed to fall over the goal line. Afterwards somebody kicked the goal that gave us the game by one point.

That was the only time in my life that I was a hero.

# CHAPTER
# TWO

I would wish to go right on telling you about a lot of fine things that I did after that, but I can't. That game was the one thing that made me shine. It was my big day. The principal of the school made a speech about me to the student body, and the girls looked sweet at my ugly mug. I deserved it all; nobody will ever know how my busted shoulder hurt me, when I was making that run.

While I lay waiting for my shoulder to get well, I had made up my mind. This was the time for me to exit from school life before I became a flivver in the mid-term examinations. When my arm could swing in the shoulder socket again, I went home.

The old man gave me a terrible reception. When he heard that I had quit school, he lit into me. I was so scared that I hit back, and that made him wild. He did a play in one act. He laid me cold — him being about twice my size and ten times my strength. When I came to, there was my mother swabbing me down and crying.

My pride was pretty badly hurt. I left home that night and hooked a ride on a train bound East, and for ten years I did about everything that a body could hope to do, from rough carpentering to boxing. Boxing was my best bet. It was the closest to football of anything that I ever found. While it wasn't quite rough-and-tumble enough to suit me, still there was something in it that I liked.

On the subject of rough-and-tumble, I would like to say right here that a lot of these boys, that get to be champions by fancy stepping and a long left, would be nothing in a free-for-all. They would be on their backs hollering for help in no time. Anyway, I was never a fancy stepper — but I had some advantages. I was fast; I could hit as hard as the next man; I could take my share of the punishment, and I was a natural welterweight. So I got along.

It was hard work but it made good money for me after I was through the preliminary stage. Finally I got signed for my shot at the championship. I think I might have got it, too — the belt and the fancy purse. But I had one bout signed between me and the big one — a roughneck by the name of McAllister. When he found that I was beating him to a pulp, he closed on me, threw me with a wrestling hold, and fell on top of me. I landed on my left shoulder.

It broke a bone — only a little one, but when it healed, I couldn't straighten my left arm. The best that I could ever do would be long-range hooking and infighting with it, after that. What is a prize fighter without a good straight left? Nothing in these scientific days where the boys fence for openings. I saw that I had to quit the ring. I had enough money to pay the doctor and $100 over. I spent that $100 buying me a ticket

West. I knew that I had had my fling. I was nearly thirty. I'd failed to set the world on fire, and I knew that the place for me to grow old and die was not in any city but out on the range. I didn't go back to my home, because me and the old man had never been friends since our fight. When it came to buying a ticket, the town that stuck in my head was Lesley Burns's home town — him that was quarterback on the Whitman eleven. His town was Arica. The queer sound of that name had always stayed in my head.

At Arica, I got off the train.

There I was on the station platform of that little town, bringing back to the range a game shoulder, $5.10 in cash, and all my worldly goods in a satchel. There was a fine rain falling, enough to turn all the lights into spangles, for it was evening.

I didn't have an overcoat, so I turned up my collar and looked around at things. There was plenty to see. Arica wasn't much. It was almost swallowed up in the hollow where it lay, but there were big mountains walking up on every side, the cow country was on the low slopes and in the valleys between the peaks, as I knew well enough. A hard country even for a cow country, where things are naturally hard, anyway. They don't grow cows where other crops will prosper.

It looked pretty fair to me, and I was about to step down from the platform and start along up the street to find a cheap hotel, when a chap came up and slapped me on the shoulder.

It was my game shoulder, so I turned around, cursing. There was Les Burns, looking as natural as you please. His hair was just as red; his face was just as thin, and he looked pretty near as young as he did the last day when I had seen him on the football field.

He said: "Well, Garver, here you are back with us again. How is everything with Kid Denver?"

I didn't like that any too well. Kid Denver was my ring name, you understand. Some folks have a little prejudice against prize fighters.

"Where did you get that?" I asked.

"Oh, I follow the sporting news. And I saw your picture. When you have your fight with the champ, my money is going to be placed on you."

"You forget that Denver stuff," I said. "I'm plain Ed Garver . . . no more and no less. That goes, Burns."

"Come, come," replied Burns, "there's no call to lose your temper. But step over to my office. You'll get wet out here."

There was nothing much better for me to do. I followed Burns across the street and up the stairs into a fine little office that had *Lesley Burns, attorney at law*, done in big black letters on the clouded glass of the door. In the outer office he told a pretty stenographer that what she was finishing up could be left till tomorrow. Then he took me on into his own room. It was very comfortable, with a big mahogany roll-top desk, a fancy carpet on the floor, easy chairs, and three windows. He set a box of cigars in front of me, saying: "Sit down. Help yourself, and tell me how the world is using you, Garver."

I bit into a good cigar that drew like a handmade beauty and had the taste that angels know. Through the blue-brown mist of the smoke I was watching Lesley Burns. He was dressed fine, in a very neat brown suit, cut just a little sporting; he had a bright check necktie on and a very high, stiff collar. He looked healthy, and he looked prosperous.

"Ever since you stopped me in that game," said Les Burns, "I've been interested in you a lot. I don't mind telling you that not many fellows have been able to stop me. I mean they didn't have the wits to figure out what I was intending to do on that play."

"Why, Burns," I said, "that play was about the best thing that I've ever done. Don't rate me by that. I knew that you wanted to smear me good in that game because I had a reputation. That made me guess that you'd carry the ball yourself, and that you'd try to score your touchdown through my position."

"All right," said Lesley Burns, "you may say that if you want to, but I have my own opinion. Now what are you up to out here in the sticks? Recuperating?"

I told him about the accident to my shoulder, and how it had spoiled my ring career.

Then he said: "I have some influence in this little old town, and I think that I could find you a good business opening. I know a fellow who wants a partner in the cigar-store business. Would you like that? I could fix a loan for your share of the business."

I stopped him right there.

"Burns, this is all amazing decent of you, but, as a matter of fact, I'm not blowing any bubbles, just now.

By nature, I was cut out for being a plain cowpuncher. I've tried my hand at other jobs. I've invested ten years and a lot of hard knocks. I've got five dollars and a game shoulder out of it. Now I'm going back on the range and see if I've forgotten how to ride a bronco without pulling leather, and how to throw a rope and bulldog a yearling. That's my style, and that's my speed. Now you know all about me."

He pursed out his mouth and studied the end of his cigar for a minute. "That's your ambition, eh?"

"Yes."

He poured himself a drink and tossed it off in a way that showed he had plenty of exercise in bending his elbow.

Then he looked up at me and right through me. He had a cold pair of eyes, when he wanted to use them. They drilled right into me.

"Look here, old-timer," he said, "I'm driving out to my ranch tonight. Suppose that you go along with me, eh?"

"You own a ranch, too?" I asked, a good deal impressed. "A lawyer and a rancher, too?"

"It sounds a good deal fancier than it really is," said Les Burns. "I'm prosperous, though. I own the town's baseball club . . . grounds, contracts, and all. No mortgage on anything. And I own the little building that this office is in. I have a neat little practice. Nothing grand, but pretty good. Besides, I have a ranch that my father left to me. Between you and me, I might do better by sticking to the ranch and letting these sidelines all drop. Because, old man, the ranch isn't doing as much as it ought to do. Not by a long sight. But I don't like country life. I like the town better. However, that shows you the way that I'm fixed. An idea pops into my mind. How would it be for you to come out there with me, look that ranch over, and see if you can get any ideas for improving the management of it?

"I make a mess of it myself, and it's hard to get a good foreman. I don't mean to say that I'm offering you the job of running the place. But I'd like to have you look over me and the ranch, while I look you over. Does that sound good to you?"

Of course, it sounded good to me. I liked everything about Les Burns. I liked his clean-cut way of going at a thing and his open hand. I liked everything about him, I might say, except the snappy sporting touch that he had. That may sound strange coming from an ex-pug, but I never liked the sporting headliners. Snappy clothes generally go along with what you may call sporty thinking. And that's really a bad kind, as nearly everybody knows.

However, we started for the ranch together.

# CHAPTER
# THREE

Set off the way it was in a hollow, it looked more like some rich man's shooting lodge than a ranch house. There were a lot of trees around it, and a brook came rippling alongside of it; it had a good-natured look, all around, that usually doesn't fit in with a ranch house. Around a ranch house there is usually just one thing of importance — that is the work with the cows. Trees are turned into firewood, and a beautiful view consists of cows, and then more cows. This place was different. You could see that when Les Burns's father started this ranch, he didn't have an eye on the dollars only.

When we drove up under the front porch, I saw that the house was what you call the cottage type — that means, it was never more than two stories high, and it scrambled all over the ground. It had a roof very sharply angled, with big eaves stretching far out from the wall — a lazy, comfortable sort of a house. You could tell that there would be all sorts of nooks and crannies on the inside — the sort of a house that a kid would like a lot, the sort of a house that even a grown-up would find new things in, to the end of his life.

**144**

Les Burns said, as we started for the front door, me carrying my satchel and he a couple of packages that he had brought out from town: "Look here, there's a friend of mine, by the name of Sam Jarvis, coming over tonight."

He seemed just a little hesitant, so he added: "I'll tell you how it is, old-timer. This Jarvis is the sort of a fellow that you're not going to like, at all. I remember that even when you were playing football and making great guns of it, you didn't like fellows who talked about themselves. That's what Jarvis does. Hardly anything but."

I thought, at the time, that it was a little queer that he should warn me about a man who was a stranger to me and who was going to be a guest in his house. That was because I hadn't met Jarvis. There was a little time for me to look over the place, from the house to the bunkhouse. Everything looked good to me. The sample of riding horses that I found in the pasture looked like the real thing to me, I can tell you. That counted more than anything else. Give me a bed made up of rocks, hot water instead of coffee, and beans three times a day for chuck — but if you have a good saddle string, you can get along with me. Well, everything looked fine.

When I finished looking things over, I said to Burns: "What sort of a set of boys have you got here?"

"Why, as 'punchers go nowadays, a mighty good set, I'd say. But nobody with enough brains to put at the head of the lot and run the outfit. Nobody with a head for cows, you understand."

"Well," I said, "I don't know exactly what you want, and I don't know just what the difficulties may be on this range. Worst of all, it's a long time since I've had herd riding to do. What I want is one month of riding with the boys, here, learning the problems and learning the men before they ever guess that I'm going to be boss. After that month, if you still think that you'd like to have me boss the place for you . . . well, I can tell you that I never saw an outfit that I liked any better at the first look."

That was how I felt, and Burns seemed to take pretty kindly to what I had to say. I was for starting with a sleep in the bunkhouse the very first night, but Burns wouldn't hear of it.

He said: "This industry stuff and newsboy-to-president stuff is all very well, but it won't buy you everything. The thing for you to do, old-timer, is to bunk in the house the first night. It's not going to be instantly fatal to your reputation with the boys to spend the first night here in the house."

I had a very queer feeling about it, and I was right. You can trust those impulses that you get — like when the instinct says that the other fellow who is looking at your jaw is really going to take a smash at your stomach. Once I dropped an elbow over my ribs and blocked an unexpected swing of the Chicago Cyclone's that would have knocked me into the middle of next week.

If I had stayed away from the house, everything would have been all right. That's just another one of those important *ifs*. You find a lot of them in this hard-luck story. If I hadn't smashed my shoulder, I would have been champion — maybe.

When I came down to dinner I found Jarvis there. Right away I could understand why Les Burns had warned me about him. He was one of those big, fat fellows, who rock back on their heels, put their hands in their trouser pockets, and show you a couple of yards of fancy vest.

This boob had on a checked vest that you could see half a mile away. He had a big gold watch chain with a Swiss movement on one end and a gold pencil on the other. He wore a high, stiff white collar with a big loose fold of flabby flesh hanging over the edge of it. His red-and-white necktie had a great big emerald stickpin in it.

He had small feet, and very tapering small white hands, so fat that there was a dimple over each knuckle. He was proud of those hands, too. He was that kind of a man — proud of everything that belonged to him. He was always laying that hand on the table and pressing it down quite flat, so that people could really have a good look at it.

When it came to talking, he loved to hear himself. When somebody else was trying to entertain, he had a blank look in his eye, so's you could see that what he was trying to do was to think up his next remark. Yes, he was a worm.

With a fellow like that, there could be a three-ring circus with a part of him in every one of the rings, and still he wouldn't be able to get all of the attention that he would like to have. You can call that sort of a fellow whatever you like; I call him low.

Right away, when he came in, he got in the center of the room, and he stood there looking things over.

"Pretty nice little old shack that you got here, Les," he said. "But me, I'm queer. I got to have a place that is my own. Couldn't live in a house that anybody else built. No, I'd have to stir out and get me a place of my own. Very funny, that way. Cost me eighty thousand dollars, that little fancy of mine!"

That was the way with this Jarvis. You've known people like that. You could start talking about the distance to Mars, and before you got through, he would be telling you how much money he had made out of something, or how much money he had spent on something.

Curse a man like that. Particularly when you only have $5 in your own pocket, and no overcoat on your back.

When he met me, he gave my hand a hard squeeze. I must say that he had plenty of muscle in spite of his fat.

He looked me right up and down. "Well, Garver, what's your line?"

"Cowpunching."

He gave a start and looked at me again. Then he smiled and turned his back on me. You could see that he wouldn't want to waste his time on a common cowpuncher. I got a terrible desire, right there, to sink a fist into him.

When we were at the table, he kept the ball rolling, as they say. In fact, he did nearly all the rolling. After dinner we sat around and had whiskey and seltzer water. I put about one drop in a whole glassful of the seltzer, and that didn't get a cheer from Jarvis.

He said: "Don't be afraid of this stuff. This is the real thing. This is good whiskey. I know, because I got it from a darn' good bootlegger and gave it to Burns. Didn't I, Les?"

Les Burns admitted that he had got it from Jarvis, then he winked at me.

"You got to have a head on you to drink whiskey, though," said Jarvis. "Me, I got the head for it. It never flusters me. I thrive on it . . . get fat on it . . . eh, Les? You know me! I tell you, Carver, that I have . . ."

"Garver is my name," I said.

I don't know why that little mistake always makes me mad, but it does, anyway. Nine people out of ten call me Carver after I've been introduced to them. It always makes me mad. Sounds like a little thing, but I don't see why folks can't tell a C from a G.

"Garver, is it?" he asked. "Well, Garver, I've put a cellar under my house with room for everything from beer to whiskey. What would you guess that it cost me to stock that cellar of mine, Carver?"

"Garver is the name," I said, getting pretty mad. "It begins with a G. Y'understand?"

"With a G, like goose, or gump, or goof, eh?" remarked Jarvis, putting back his head while he laughed and laughed at that weak-kneed joke that wouldn't have brought a smile from a congregation of half-wits. "Well, sir, I'll tell you what. I have fifteen hundred dollars in whiskey alone, in that cellar of mine, and the whole shebang cost me a shade over sixty-five hundred dollars."

"*Humph!*" I replied.

"It's a fact, Mister Carver. My friend Burns will bear me out. He's been through that cellar, and sampled some of the good stuff . . . eh, Les? Tell Carver if I've lied about it."

"Garver!" I yelled at him.

"Oh, the devil with that name," said Jarvis. "I can't be bothered with the little names of little people."

I would have asked him to step outside with me, right then, but Les Burns stood up and walked over to me. He poured a couple of fingers of whiskey into my glass.

"Take it easy. He means no harm," whispered Burns.

I was so mad that I swallowed about half of that glass. Right away, my head began to sing. If I'd had my wits about me, I would have noticed what I was doing, but my attention was too thoroughly occupied with that idiot, Jarvis. That stuff never agreed with me. I had to cut it out while I was in training, and I got in the habit of doing without it.

# CHAPTER
# FOUR

After a minute, Jarvis snapped open the face of his watch. "Ten o'clock," he said. "About time for us to have our little talk, old-timer, isn't it?"

"I'll say good night, then," I said.

"Oh, wait a minute," broke in Burns. "I don't think that it's more than a quarter to . . . not by my watch."

"Your watch, eh?" said Jarvis. "Does it keep time?"

"Of course. Very accurate, I think."

"What did you pay for it?"

"Seventy-five, I think."

Jarvis stood there juggling his watch in his hand and smiling contemptuously down at Les Burns.

"I'll tell you what mine cost me. Four . . . hundred . . . and . . . thirty-eight dollars . . . and . . . fifty cents! Marked down from six hundred."

"The devil it did," said Les Burns.

"The devil it didn't! Take a look at it."

Burns took the watch, but, just before he could examine it, there was a rap at the door. In came a brown-faced cowpuncher.

"Hello, Granger," said Burns. "What's up? Come right in."

"I ain't gonna bother you, Mister Burns," said Granger. "All I want to say is that Gypsy Ogden was due back from town by suppertime, at the latest, and he ain't showed up yet. What d'you want me to do with him?"

"Is Gyp on a bat again?" asked Burns.

"It looks that way."

"Why, if he comes back full of liquor, fire him on the spot, Granger, or else wait till he sobers up a little and let him have it in the morning. I'm tired of putting up with this booze fighting. Is that all?"

"That's all. Good night."

Granger backed out of the door.

I never dreamed, then, how much that was to mean to me later on — just knowing the name of Gypsy Ogden. At the time, of course, I didn't think anything about it. Jarvis filled up my glass again when I wasn't looking.

"Have another shot at this stuff, kid," he said. "It'll do you good."

I got mad again. Being called Kid Denver in the ring never made anybody popular that called me Kid in private life. I was about to spout out something pretty nasty, but I choked it back and took another long drink to keep my hands busy. Then my head spun around worse than ever.

There was something else to take my attention this time, though. Les Burns was fooling with the watch and nodding his head over it. It was certainly a beauty. Hardly thicker than half a finger, and you couldn't hear it *tick*, it was so smooth. Now he snapped open the back of it to have a look at the action, and the minute it was open, he give a start.

"Where did you pick this up?" he asked, very sharp.

"Where d'you think? On the street?" asked Jarvis, grinning.

"I'm asking you."

"Sort of rides you, doesn't it? Well, kid, I'm sorry to step on your toes. But you know how it is. Everything is fair in love and war. Well, old kid, she's mine."

"Kate Mullen!" gasped out Burns, and you could see that he was hard hit. He even turned white and had to set his teeth. The hand that held the watch shook until the highlight on the gold case shivered and glanced from side to side.

"Kate Mullen is the girl," said Jarvis. "I looked them all over, and Kate Mullen is the girl for me. Looked over the whole county, and there ain't a thing to touch her for looks, action, or brains. She's a knock-out, and that's the kind of a girl that I want to put in to run that big new house of mine."

You just wouldn't believe that there was such a fathead in the whole world.

Les Burns handed over the watch without saying a word, and what does this rotter, Jarvis, do but cart the watch across to me, and hand it to me with the back open.

"There she is, kid. Have a look at her and tell me if she ain't a dinger."

I expected to see the face of some pretty little blockhead — but it wasn't that kind of a face. Darned sensible girl she looked — no beauty, but very pretty, with a good big pair of eyes and plenty of room between them. She was the sort of a girl that any man with a head on his shoulders would look at twice. Here she was picked off by a dumbbell like this. It made me sick.

"Listen to that watch, kid," said Jarvis. "Did you ever have anything that run as smooth as that in your life?"

I shouldn't have done it. I've got no excuses to offer — except that it was the whiskey that was in my head at the time, and I have to admit that booze isn't any excuse. I knew that I couldn't stand whiskey, which was all the more reason that I should have kept away from it. But I *didn't*. I went in and took my share.

When I listened to that fool Jarvis, talking this way, something snapped in me. A flood of hot blood rushed into my head, and I reached back and snapped out a big Colt.

"Yes," I said. "I have something that runs as smooth as that and keeps straight time, too. Here it is!"

I said that as I whipped out that gun and shoved the muzzle of it into him. He jumped pretty near halfway across the room, and Les Burns, white in the face, jumped up and grabbed me, saying: "Old-timer, put that away. Has a bit of whiskey gone straight to your head?"

I was ashamed, and I would have told them so — but Jarvis didn't give me a chance. He came charging right up the minute that the gun was out of sight.

"Take that gun away from him, Les," he said. "I'm going to give the little rat a dressing down."

154

"Shut up, Jarvis," said Burns. "Garver is a buzz saw. He would tear you in two. Let him alone, Jarvis. He simply can't stand this stuff."

"No," said Jarvis, throwing off his coat and unveiling a pair of shoulders that a stevedore would have been proud of. "No, I won't leave him alone. I don't care how much of a buzz saw he may be. I won't stand for any man pulling a gun and shoving it into my face."

He was terrible brave, you see, and the nearer that he got to me and the more he looked down on me, and saw how much bigger he was than me, the more revengeful and high-spirited he got.

It disgusted me, of course. It made me angry, too. Being a prize fighter, a man has to take a lot from the other fellow. If you hit him, the boys pass a bad word around about you and let it be known everywhere that you take advantage of your training in the ring to beat up fellows who haven't the science.

I said to Les Burns: "You keep that sap off of me, and I'll go to bed real peaceful. I'm sorry that I shoved a gun at him, but the face of that girl was . . ."

"I know," whispered Burns. "But now, go to bed and forget about it. I know. Run along, Garver."

He started me for the door.

I was unsteady on my pins — that fool whiskey had got to me so bad. When big Jarvis saw that, he figured that I was helpless. Nothing could hold him, then. He rushed up to us, tore Les Burns away, and made a pass at me.

I wasn't so foggy that that big ham could have hit me with a ten-foot pole. I ducked under his arm while it

155

was swinging like a gate. As I straightened, I hit right in the fattest bulge of his checked vest. It was like punching a half-empty balloon. He fell on his face, knocked cold.

Les Burns let out a groan.

"You've killed him! He'll raise the devil with me, for this."

"I'm sorry," I said. "But he ain't hurt bad. He's too well padded to be hurt bad. I'm sorry that I hit him, Les, but you know how it was."

"You go up the stairs and go to bed," said Les, pointing a finger at me. "You go right up . . . if you can walk straight."

I wasn't as bad as all of that. I managed my way up the stairs pretty good, but when I got to my room, it was closer and warmer than the living room. I didn't have sense enough to open the window to let in more fresh air. I thought that I would lie down on the bed for a little while until my head cleared up a bit. You know how it is. You close your eyes for one wink, and, when you wake up, it's morning with somebody beating at the door.

When I woke up, it was a good deal later; there was a queer *humming* in my ears and a far-away feeling. My tongue was swollen, and my brains were all dizzy. There wasn't any knocking at the door, and there wasn't any voice calling me — only a hand touching my shoulder, and a voice that was whispering.

A whisper is the ugliest sound in the world, when it wants to be. It has it all over the *hissing* of a snake; the kind of a whisper that I heard was that sort of a thing.

**156**

It was saying: "Garver, Garver . . . for heaven's sake . . . what've you done? Wake up. Wake up."

I opened my eyes. Through the haze, I could see my friend, Les Burns, standing in the middle of the light of the lamp that he was carrying. He was dressed in pajamas, and he was staring at me as though I was a fire-breathing dragon, or something like that.

"What's up? What's biting you, partner?" I asked.

He backed away with a jump that made the flame leap in the throat of the lamp chimney. Then he blinked and put the lamp down on the table.

"Well, has something happened?"

Burns moistened his white lips before he could answer.

"You don't remember?" he said.

"That I hit the fat stiff? Yes, I remember that. Has he turned out bad? Did I reach his liver, or something? I thought that my fist would never stop traveling."

He brushed all of that idea away.

"Never mind the hitting . . . never mind the biting," he said. "That's nothing . . . that's nothing at all. But . . . good heaven. Garver . . ."

"Talk out," I said. "Stop that whispering, or I'll go crazy."

"You fool. You fool," he gasped out at me. "Do you know what you're saying? No, you don't."

He looked around him, very wild.

"Ah! Here it is!"

And he reached over and picked up something from the middle of the floor — something long and black and glittering — my Colt.

# CHAPTER
# FIVE

That brought my wits back to me with a jump, and I stood up in the middle of the floor with an exclamation, asking Les Burns what the devil it all meant. He backed away from me quickly and looked as though he wanted to run away.

He said in a soothing but frightened way: "Take it easy now, old man. *I'm* your friend. I mean no harm to you."

"All right," I said, "but give me my Colt, and stop pointing it at me that way, will you?"

I started to walk up to him, but Burns flattened his back against the door and thrust out the gun at full arm's length. There was no doubt about him having a dead bead on me, and I knew that there was danger in him.

He said: "You come an inch nearer me, and I'll shoot you, Garver!"

I stopped, of course, and took a jump backwards.

"What's eating you?" I yelled at him. "Why, man . . ."

"All right," said Les Burns. "I mean friendly by you, but I don't trust you, and you know that I've got good reason not to trust you."

**158**

"You don't trust me? Because I hit that fat loafer that was . . ."

"Because you hit him? D'you think I'm going back to *that* old story?" asked Les Burns with a sort of a sneer.

"What in the world have I done in my sleep?" I asked at last. "Outside of slugging that big Chinaman, I've done nothing wrong since I came to this house."

"In your sleep," muttered Les Burns, and the idea seemed to sink in on his brain pretty strong. Then he shook his head and said: "It can't be."

"Will you tell me what you're talking about, before I go crazy?"

"Garver," he said, "walk ahead of me. It may be that you mean what you say, and, if you do, this is the worst tragedy that I've ever heard about. Walk ahead of me down the hall, and I'll tell you which way to turn. Mind you, I'll be watching you close all the time. Don't try anything, Garver. You've proved that you're a dangerous customer this night, but if you try anything fancy on me, I'll prove that I'm every bit as bad as you are."

I didn't make any answer. This tangle was getting so bad that I thought I would go bad unless I found out what it was all about.

He kept guiding me along the hall to the farther end of the house. There he made me turn through a door and into a room where the bedclothes had been pulled off the bedstead and onto the floor, as if they'd been dragged off in the death agony of the man that had been sleeping there. Right in the middle of the clothes, with his arms thrown over his head, was big Jarvis, with a great spot of blackened red along one side of his face.

I just gave it one look, and then I turned away and leaned against the wall.

"Les," I said, "tell me quick. Are you accusing me of doing this?"

"Old-timer," he said, "there's a chamber of this Colt that's empty."

"Let me have it."

"I'm a fool to do it, I suppose," he said, "but . . . I can't distrust you now that I see you. Here's your gun, Garver."

I took that gun and looked it over. There was no doubt about one chamber of it being discharged, and there was no doubt about me having seen Les Burns pick that gun up from the floor of my room. It made me sick and dizzy; I could only stand there and shake my head.

I said: "I didn't do it, old man. I swear to you . . . on my honor, before God as my judge . . . that I didn't do it."

Les Burns brushed both of his hands away from him, as though he would try to dispose of what I had said in that way, and he answered: "Take this mighty easy. Try to clear your head. I believe you, Garver. I've seen you play on the football field, and I don't believe that you're the kind of a man to sneak into a man's bedroom at night and murder him while he lies reading. I don't believe that you would do any such thing. It isn't in you. But I ask you to try to clear your memory and get back, not to what you know in your conscious mind, but what might have happened while you were asleep."

It was a mighty bad thing to try to do. While I stood there with my head bent, struggling with myself, I heard him say: "Tell me, honest. Did you ever sleepwalk in your life before?"

"No."

"Take another think," he said.

I did think it over, and then I actually remembered that once, when I was a kid, I had waked up with my hand on the cold balustrade, going down the stairs in our house. When I told Les Burns about that, I thought that the eyes would pop right out of his head.

"That explains everything," he said. "But now can't you try to remember what might have happened this night. Don't you recall sneaking down the hall? Surely you must remember walking into that lighted room . . . and, most of all, you must recollect that you pulled the trigger, and the gun roared . . . look here . . . so close to his head that the flame blackened and smoked his face."

I couldn't look close enough to see that. I was too sick.

"Tell me one other thing," said Les Burns. "What was the last time that you did any drinking to speak of?"

"About seven years ago."

"Seven years!" gasped out Les Burns. "You mean to say that you've not . . ."

"I may have had a glass of beer once or twice, but not enough to . . ."

He put both his hands over his head.

"It's my fault," he muttered. "The booze did it. And you didn't want to take it. Partner, I'm really the man that's to blame for this murder."

There was a *thumping* knock at the front door of the house.

"They've come to inquire . . . the 'punchers have come from the bunkhouse to find out the meaning of that shot and yell."

"Was there a yell?" I gasped out.

"Didn't you hear even that?" He simply turned blue as he asked it. Then he said: "Old-timer, tell me quick. Do you want to see this thing through, or will you take my advice and beat it? I tell you, Jarvis was a pretty well-known man in this county, and it might give you a pretty rough jury . . . on sleepwalking and whiskey, I mean."

I saw what he meant. I had been drinking too much whiskey for the strength of my head. I had walked in my sleep — I had no memory of having done such a thing — but a bullet was found gone, and the barrel of my gun was warm.

Then, in a flash, I thought of the other things that could be brought up, and that *would* be brought up. I thought of the way it would be pointed out how I had differed with Jarvis and made a foolish scene about the way he called me by the wrong name. Then I thought about how I had been actual fool enough to draw a revolver on him because he disgusted me. That showed how much a sip or two of whiskey had unbalanced me.

Worst of all, I had actually struck Jarvis hard enough to knock him down and out.

Everything was all built up, and I could see some cheap district attorney getting up in front of a hick jury and pointing to my reputation as a prize fighter — which was always against a man in a pinch like that — and then telling how I had deliberately walked down the hall with my gun and . . .

It takes a good while to tell about these things, but I can give you my word that the thinking of them didn't take more than the quarter part of a full-size second. I saw what I was heading for, before the boys on the verandah had time to rap a second time.

"Les Burns," I said, "will you be a friend to me?"

"I've got two hundred dollars in my pocket," he said. "It's yours. Go as fast and as far as that will help you."

I took that money, and I shoved it in my pocket without even another thought. Then I said: "Hold them away from upstairs for a minute, Les. I'll sneak back to the corral. I need about five minutes to find a saddle and to get onto a horse."

He nodded, and I started for a back window, while he ran down the stairs, where the boys were knocking. A hollering was beginning.

When I got to the back window, I had trouble working the latch of it free. I was still working when the front door lock turned with a *snap*, and, as the door *creaked* open, I heard Les Burns singing out: "Thank heavens that you've come, boys! There's been a murder here, and, if you hadn't come in time, I might have been killed, too. Head for the back of the house. I think that he went that way when he heard you knock."

Low and mean? Yes, it was, but I never figured Les Burns for anything high class. His eyes was set too close together for that. He was too smart and too tricky. However, you could hardly blame an insect like him. First thing that you knew, unless he raised a howl, somebody might accuse him of the killing, or at least of conniving at the escape of the real murderer. I hadn't the least doubt that Les Burns meant well by me. He was simply saving his own miserable hide.

Understanding why he acted that way didn't make it any easier for me. I shook my fist into the darkness behind me and cursed them good and proper. Then I worked that window up and slid out into the night. There was a long drop, but I was too mad and excited to care much what happened to me.

I dropped safe enough, and headed away for the corrals.

# CHAPTER
## SIX

I got to them in a pretty fast sprint, and found the shed with the saddles and bridles. I grabbed what I wanted, feeling so nervous and excited that I dropped the saddle a couple of times while I was heading out toward the corral.

Just as I heaved myself over the fence, and just as the horses milled together in the center of the corral, scared of me, I heard an outbreak of yelling from the outside of the house. The cowpunchers were after me.

When I shook out my rope, you can lay to it that the sound of their voices didn't steady my hand none. The darned lariat got tangled in a knot, but the second time it came clean. I wondered whether I would have forgotten everything that I ever knew about handling a rope — which was never any too much.

There was a mite of luck for me. That rope shot fair and fine through the air. Instead of it dropping on the head of a big brown horse that I had picked out, the brown jumped clear, and a little measly gray mare shoved her head into the noose like a fool. I groaned through my set teeth, but there wasn't any time to make changes. I worked like a madman, handing myself up that rope and manning that horse. Then I got the bridle onto her head, but there wasn't any time for the saddling. There wasn't any time for anything, except to skin onto the back of that horse and hope that the cowpunchers that were coming wouldn't shoot too straight by starlight.

I could see them swarming in on the far side of the fence — looking like jumping black shadows. The swirling of the other horses around the corral covered me from them for a minute. Even after they saw me, they couldn't shoot without danger of bringing down some of the mustangs. They scattered along the fence on each side, to keep me from getting away.

By this time, I was on the back of that gray runt. I didn't know whether or not she could jump or would jump. Being on her bare back, I was at a pretty big handicap, but there wasn't anything else for it. I had to master her as well as I was able without spurs or quirt or stirrups or saddle. As I put her at the fence, it lifted up above me high and black as a gallows. It seemed to blot out half the stars. I smashed my heels into the flank of that mare, and she give a grunt and reared up.

I thought that she was refusing, and that would be the end of me, because, along the fence, I could see the cowpunchers scooting, and the twinkling of the stars on their polished guns. She didn't refuse; she reared, jumped, and cleared that fence up without flicking so much as the tip of a heel against it. There was I on the far side, with the black of the night, and the safety of the night ahead of me — if only I could sink myself deep enough and quick enough into it.

A dozen guns seemed to roar at once.

I'd used a Colt times enough, though I was never an expert. The difference in shooting at a target and in being the target yourself is more than you would hardly guess. The roar of those guns was like cannons in my ears. I flattened myself along the back of the gray, give myself up for a dead man, and shook the bridle loose.

Well, sir, I was nearly knocked off the back of that mare — not by bucking, but by the speed with which she got under way. She went off like a trained sprinter from the post, and I nearly slid off over her tail. I would have slid off, only I managed to get a couple of fingers wound into her mane when I felt myself sliding. By that I pulled myself back on just as she came to another fence.

She didn't slow up. She went over it like a greyhound after a rabbit. As she landed, I did, too — shot clean off, and landed head over heels.

Bless that little gray. If she didn't slow up right there and let me pick up myself, groggy and half gone, and drag myself onto her back again.

If those cowpunchers had followed me, of course, they would have had me dead to rights, right there. They didn't follow — I learned later — because they'd seen me flash away on Gray Maggie, and they felt that there was no use trying anything but a slow trail after me — because they knew the mare better than I did.

I knew her before morning, though. She was as gentle as a lamb, so neat-footed that I knew she was a cutting horse, and as long-winded as she was fast. I'm no heavyweight, so I didn't need any giant to carry me along. Though she had looked tiny to begin with, before she had packed me a mile, I knew that she was big enough for any work that I could ever expect out of a horse.

She was a jim-dandy, and don't you make any mistake about it. No thoroughbred strain in her — just mustang, pure and simple. Ugly-headed, roach-backed, and scrawny-necked — but though she was put together plumb careless, the materials were the best in the world, and they stood up under the strain. She had strains coming to her, poor old girl — more strains than I ever could have expected to give her.

I went toward the mountains that night, and I headed south, because the wind had turned pretty cold. South seemed the most neighborly direction. There was plenty of moisture in that rain, too. It was a fine sprinkle at first, but, as soon as the night saw what was up, and that I was trying to run away from the long arm of the law, it just turned loose and begun to slosh down buckets and buckets of water at my head.

Drenched to the skin, I began to get cold and numb. As the dawn began, I was the worst-looking and the worst-feeling drowned rat that you ever heard of in your born days. When a man feels like that — and there's nothing worse than being wet and cold — he doesn't care particularly what he does. I stopped in at the first house I came to after dawn. When I saw the chimney smoking, I rode for it, and I went in and I sat down by the stove. The woman came in with a bucket of milk and gave a squeal.

She ran out, and pretty soon along came her husband, toting a rifle and looking pretty mean. He was a long drawn-out, hard-boiled fellow with a face the color of tanned hide.

"What might you be wanting here, stranger?" he asked.

I leaped over and yanked a Colt out of its pocket and covered him. I wasn't flustered a bit; I was so cold, so hungry, and so mean, that I didn't much care whether I killed him, or he killed me.

"I want a slicker, a saddle, a good pair of spurs, another Colt, a rifle, plenty of ammunition, a pack of bacon, salt, flour, matches, and such-like stuff. I'm gonna detain you right here while your wife gets these things all together."

He looked me in the eye. I never thought that I could stand and hold up a man, like that, without dropping my chin right on my breast for shame. It was queer that I didn't feel any shame at all. When he looked at me, I looked right back at him, through his cold gray eyes and down to the bottom of his soul. While I looked, I could feel my upper lip beginning to curl and my trigger finger begin to pull — all of itself. He saw, too; his eyes lost their cold look and opened up fast enough for me to see that he was almost scared to death. He let out a yell: "Maria!"

Maria came to the outside of the door.

"Oh, Jake," she said, whining. "You ain't killed him, did you?"

"You old fool," he said, pretty impolite, "you light out and get together a saddle and a slicker and a side of bacon . . ."

And he went down through the list.

"Sit down and rest yourself," I said, "and maybe that rifle that you're toting will be good enough for me, too."

He laid the gun on the floor and excused himself from sitting down, because he said that he felt more comfortable and at home when he was standing up. I reached that rifle over to me with a jerk of my heel, and then fetched it up into my hands.

It was a good gun — not very new, but well kept, used plenty, but not badly worn. For my part, I'd rather have an old, tried gun than a new one. An old gun in good hands is one that hadn't developed any bad faults; otherwise it wouldn't have been kept in use. A new gun may work out very bad.

I liked the feel of that Winchester, and I told Jake about it. By the time I got through with looking over the gun, my pack was collected, because that Maria was about the fastest-working woman that I had ever seen. I had put the things on the back to Gray Maggie, and I walked Jake out of the house in front of me. He was pretty scared, and he kept asking me under his breath if I meant to rob him and then take him away and murder him? I didn't answer, because I thought that using his imagination for a little while wouldn't hurt him any.

We got to the top of the next hill. There I told him to cut lose and leg it for home, and not to show his head outside of his shack till noon. He turned and fairly ran for his shack. I almost expected that he would do what I told him about staying inside of it. He wasn't a coward. I mean, he had as much courage as most; he was just a sensible man.

**170**

A funny thing about this whole business was that I was in dead serious earnest from the beginning to the end of it. When I had used to read in the newspaper about some chap busting loose from prison and walking around the countryside making trouble, holding people up, and waving his guns around, promiscuous, I had always figured out that they must be bluffing. Nobody could really mean to kill folks so careless and thoughtless as the outlaws always pretended that they would. When I had a chance to see this thing working in myself, it was a mighty lot different.

I was simply too miserable to care what happened. I wanted to get a feed and warm clothes and the rest, and I started to get what I wanted. If Jake had raised a hand or made a fighting move, I would have drilled a hole clean through him. There wasn't any doubt about that; he knew it, too. That was why he couldn't look me in the eye.

Just then I was a wild beast, and he was a tame one. That made all the difference in the world. You can stand in front of the bars of the tiger's cage, and look him down, pretty easy. Suppose you were to turn a corner in a jungle and see him crouched in front of you, slavering with hunger and wagging his tail with anger. Who would have the steadiest eye, then? There was a good deal of the same difference here. Not that I want to compare myself to a tiger, you understand.

I rode on to the next hillock. There I made me a fire, cooked the grub that I had stolen, and ate it. I'm ashamed to say that, having stolen it, it tasted all the better; it was the best meal that I ever ate in my whole life.

After I had finished things up and cleaned up the tins, I seen Gray Maggie toss up her head. Down the valley five men were riding.

At any ordinary time, I wouldn't have thought anything about it, except that they were a bunch of cowpunchers out hunting for strays, or something like that. Things were changed with me, and, when I looked them all over, it didn't take me long to see that they were looking for only one stray. That stray was me!

# CHAPTER
# SEVEN

By that first look I knew some other pretty useful things, too. I knew, for instance, that there was not a horse in the lot that could give Gray Maggie a fair workout on the flat. Now that Gray Maggie was rested, and those horses had been plugging along hard and fast all the way, I knew that all I had to do was to jog right away from them.

When they saw me, and came charging, quirting their horses along and yelling their heads off like fool Indians, it irritated me a good deal, I'm here to state. I didn't feel like running at all. I was so mad at that bunch of five for hurrying me with the end of my breakfast, and I stood up there in plain view, and, when they got in good easy range and were beginning to pot shoot at me, I pulled that Winchester of Jake's to my shoulder and took a sight down the barrel.

It was a pretty sight to see them scatter away from before that gun. It was one of the prettiest things in the world to see the way they pitched to each side and scrambled for rocks. I waited until they were under cover, and then I began to get Gray Maggie ready.

They were shooting from rests, and they weren't a terrible long distance away. It gave me a lot of pleasure to stand up there and hear the bullets singing. They must have had a shooting fever, not to be able to hit me. Somehow, I *knew* that they would have the fever. I could guess that not one of them had probably ever shot at a man before, and they wouldn't be apt to be any too cool when they drew their beads at me now. They weren't. Not one of those bullets came within three feet of me. I finally got on Gray Maggie, turned around in the saddle, and waved my hat to them, then I rode off up the valley.

It doesn't take much to tickle some men when they're off by themselves; at least, it didn't take much to content me. Bluffing those five fellows out of their saddles without firing a shot, and letting them sow a whole mountainside with lead without so much as wasting a single shot on them, pleased me a good deal. All through that day, I couldn't help chuckling a good deal.

I started drifting down the back of those mountains, and I kept traveling for more than three weeks. I never left the ridge of the water divide unless I got hungry for a change of provisions, or for more of the same kind. Then I would sashay off down the first handy valley.

Most folks like to do their crooked work in the night, but I did not care when it was. When the mood rose up in me, I went and took what I wanted. Let me tell you, it was easy, because I was mean all the way through. When I knocked at a gent's door, and he came to answer it, he didn't need more than one look at my eyes to tell that I was such bad medicine that I would be about as bad as poison. After that first look, I would walk in and take a stand in a corner where I would have the walls on two sides of me. Then I would get some member of the family — I didn't care whether it was a girl or a boy, husband or wife — and I would make him sit down in front of me. I would tell him that, if he moved, or that if anybody else in the house tried any funny play, the first thing that I shot would be the person directly in front of me.

You would be surprised to hear how well that worked. I've gone into a house with seven or eight men in call of it, and I've taken what I wanted, walked out, and got away without so much as a single shot fired at me.

The worst part of this game was that it was exciting enough to make it worthwhile for its own sake, not just because I was hungry for some sort of chuck, or an overcoat, or some such thing.

The most amusing thing was the papers. You would be surprised what a lot they would write about me. They got hold of my ring history, and, of course, that was nuts for them. They wrote me up big and bold and very flattering — oh, terrible flattering. Of course, an outlaw is a hero, and the newspapers love him almost to death. You take a sneaking murderer that kills and then hides himself — what can an editor do but call him a rat and a lot of other bad names and talk about suppressing the crime wave, you understand? It's a good deal different with an outlaw that goes out and lives on the folks that are hunting him down. An outlaw like that is valuable copy.

One time I rode down into Creightonville, that little Colorado crossroads town, and I sat down there in a corner and made the proprietor of the hotel read aloud to me, while his cook brought in ham and eggs and coffee, and every other good thing that you could pretty nearly name.

The proprietor took it very easy and hauled out some papers and begun to read the accounts of what I had done. Really I had to blush. The reporters told about me being one of the greatest boxers and fighters that had ever adorned the squared circle. They told about me being a warrior but a gentleman. And all the rest of the bunk. Well, I had to stop that man from reading any more.

"But it's all true, old-timer," he said to me.

"It's a string of lies," I answered.

"Garver," he said, "don't tell me that. I was a mite wild when I was a boy myself. Maybe another wrong would have barred me out. Besides, everybody knows that it was the booze that made you kill Jarvis, and not anything in your right mind."

There you are. The papers had the whole countryside so hypnotized that they head-hunted me on the one hand while on the other hand that same crew of head-hunters was slapping me on the back.

What I want to point out is that I wasn't worth this fuss. I wasn't any hero. I was a mean, low, dangerous, bad actor, who had figured that the world had crowded me into a corner, and I was ready to fight back like a cornered rat. There wasn't anything graceful or kind about me; there wasn't anything generous about me, either. Those idiot papers talked about me as though I was a sort of a knight errant. It was ridiculous. The one part of my life that I'm really ashamed of is that roaming around through the mountains, hating everybody and robbing right and left. I've done other bad things, but they could be excused, in a way.

Then the papers began to make a great flare about the fact that I had never fired a gun since the hunt for me began. That set them all off again. Every time I went down to the cabin of some poor sucker and made him give me a meal of hot cakes and bad coffee, the papers would flare out with headlines about the desperado making another raid without firing a shot.

To hear them talk, you would think I carried lightning in my eye, and that folks just curled up and quit cold, when I came along. I want to be modest, but I may as well be truthful and admit that they *did* start curling up when I showed my face. The newspapers had published that face, so that the farthest mining camps had seen it. Everybody in the farthest nooks and crannies of the mountains had read yards and yards of copy about what a terrible deadly fighter I was.

There's no doubt that you can hypnotize folks into nearly anything. I suppose I was one of the worst shots that ever galloped a horse. Just because I was able to get by on bluff, and never had to show how bad a shot I really was, I got to be famous.

As I was saying, I finished my trip south along the ridge of the mountains. Then I turned north, and I thought that it would be rather a lark to see whether I could break right back through the same district where

I had been before. I made a long ride the first night and finished it off by sloping back to one of the places where I had stopped on my way down.

The next day I did the same thing; the third day the papers were flaming with it — that I was going back as I had come and stopping at the same houses — to show the sheriffs how ridiculous and inefficient they really were.

# CHAPTER
# EIGHT

I had not had the slightest idea of sticking to such a program, of course, but the newspapers put the fool idea into my head, and I did that very thing. To think of the danger that I went through makes me sick, now. For a whole week I went back, stopping at every house where I had called on the southern trip. On the eighth day, as I came close to a little cabin where I had been before, the whole hedge of young fir trees near the place turned into fire and smoke. I think there must have been a dozen or fifteen men with rifles there. Every rifle was a repeater, and every repeater was emptying its magazine at me as fast as shells could be ejected and triggers pulled.

Pulling Gray Maggie around, I rode diagonally across their field of fire and away. When I was out of sight, they came crashing after me, with fresh horses to carry them along. I could never outdistance them with a tired mare under me, but I managed to get Maggie out of their sight. Then I jumped her into a thicket and dismounted. We stood like a pair of scared rabbits, watching that procession go smashing by, yelling and cheering and swearing that I must be full of lead, and that they would surely find my dead body along the way, before long.

When they were gone, I turned and rode straight back to the cabin behind the young line of firs. When I went in, I found nobody but the woman of the place and her two young children. They were frightened to death when they saw me. When I sat down and smiled at them, they got up a little courage again. I had them cook me a good meal, and I borrowed a pound of tobacco from the stock of the man of the house, while his wife swore to me that he had had nothing to do with setting the trap for me.

Of course, I didn't believe her, but I felt no malice. I was pretty much at peace with the world, that night, for, as I sat there in the lamplight of the kitchen, I counted one bullet hole through the crown of my hat and three more through my coat, where it had flapped wide in the wind as I galloped away from those riflemen.

Why they had not killed me a dozen times over, you may say was due to the starlight, the speed of Gray Maggie, and the excitement of those fellows who were lying there in wait for me. As a matter of fact, on that night as I sat in the kitchen and saw where the bullet had combed through my clothing, I figured that there was something more than chance connected with it. I'd never been a religious man, and I'm not religious down to this day and hour, but I couldn't help feeling that there was some power that governed the life and death of a man, and that power wasn't ready for me to die.

180

I went back into the hills and spent three days taking it easy, and getting over the shock of that affair. Then I started in where I left off. They laid half a dozen more traps for me on my route, but I managed to escape from each one. The trouble with their schemes was always that they took too many pains and wouldn't be content to put just one or two men in a shack where they expected me. They always wanted at least a dozen, to make sure of the desperado, and the more times I fooled them, the more men they wanted to trap me.

You can't put fifteen men or so under a hat. I could always sneak around a cabin for a little while and make out whether or not the trap was set. Then I would wait nearby until they gave up hope of me. When they started out to scout through the mountains to find a trace of me, I would slip into the town or the house, whichever it might be, get what I wanted, and then go on.

After a week of that foolish danger dodging, I began to pick up the newspaper accounts of that expedition of mine. The editors were simply busting themselves. They put their emphasis on two things. The first one was that I hadn't fired a bullet, as yet; the second was that I hadn't skipped, on the return journey, a single house where I had appeared on the way down.

It made a great game for me, and pretty amusing reading. Every article that appeared in a paper made the sheriff groan and cuss and set his teeth and swear harder than ever that he would capture me. Of course, the more he set his teeth, the easier it was for me to slip through the net. The more determined they got, the more obvious were all the tricks that they tried, until finally I finished the last stage of my journey. I was in the cabin of Jake and Maria, as big as life, and Jake and Maria were looking at me as though I was a ghost.

The decent people always treated me pretty well, and they would always talk to me about what I had been doing, even joke with me about the sheriff, his posses, and his traps. The low-down people were always mean and hard, watching me like rats watching a cat. It was that way with Jake and Maria.

Jake said, when I got up to leave: "I suppose that the next place you visit will be the house where you . . ."

"Jake, what you talking about?" muttered Maria, snarling.

"The house where I murdered Jarvis?" I asked. "Well, maybe that will be my next stop. How did the boys fail to come here to wait for me?"

"They were here all yesterday and the day before," said Jake, "as most likely you know. Then they gave it up and decided that you wouldn't be fool enough to try this place. They rode away, all of them, though I warned the pack that they were acting like idiots."

I knew that he was right, because I had been lying up in a little dugout on the brow of the hill for two days, waiting for the pack to clear out of Jake's house and let me in. I asked Jake if there was another trap laid for me at the house of Les Burns. He told me that he didn't know — but that he hoped so.

He couldn't help letting his malice out just that much, and I hardly blamed him. The things that I had taken from him amounted to a good deal in his miserly eyes.

When I rode off, I turned around in the saddle and promised Jake that, if I ever laid my hands on any money, I would sure pay him the face value of everything that I had taken. At that, he merely laughed in a high, whining tone, through his nose. There was nothing but meanness in that man, no trust for anybody, and no interest in anything but himself.

After that, I went off by myself and spent a whole week living rough and free and easy in the upper peaks. It was the middle of summer — cool up yonder, but not freezing cold except at night. There was all the game that I could want for. I had salt and flour and bacon and coffee, which was all prime. When I wanted venison or bear, I could take a dip down into the first valley that I came to, and just lie there and wait for game to come along.

It was an easy life, and yet not a lazy one, because when a man is being hunted with a price on his head — and a good, fat price, at that — you would be surprised to know how he feels. I had more or less got used to it by this time, but I could never stop being watchful.

Have you ever had a chance to watch a grizzly go through the hills? While I was off there in the mountains, I've had an opportunity to train my glass on a grizzly more than once, to see him sneaking along on a trail. He would be hunting for something, a beehive, or roots, or a wounded deer — or almost anything that would fit comfortably into his big stomach. That grizzly would have nothing to fear in the world in the way of other animals. He could smash half a dozen wolves to smithereens; he could break every rib in the side of a mountain lion with a single smash of his paw — but he had to look out for man. That made him so cautious that it would have surprised you. Even when the wind was coming straight and steady toward him, he would pause at each rise of the ground, and scout around and examine the other side of the slope before he would venture over. Every noise that happened anywhere near him would make him run for cover; every quick scent would make him rear on his hind legs. Every time he moved, he kept his eyes wandering around on the edges of the sky.

I got to be the same way — no exaggerating. I couldn't eat three mouthfuls at a meal without shifting and looking over my shoulder. I never slept more than a couple of hours at a time, without waking up and taking a survey around me. Usually, at night, I kept awake almost from dark to dawn. It was in the afternoon, in the dimness of the morning, and in the evening, that I did my sleeping. I wouldn't trust mere darkness to shelter me from my enemies. I was more willing to trust my ears and my eyes to warn me if some enemy was coming near to me. Maybe this seems to be a queer, jumpy, unhappy sort of life to you.

Right now I hardly know how to explain it. It was pretty miserable to be away from any friend and to have no companions at all. Just the same, I have to say that I was pretty happy all the time. Being wide awake was fun. To this day I'm not such a solid sleeper as I once was — and I'm glad of it.

It was a great game to play, as I was doing, against the law, and all of the power that the law has behind it. I had only myself and my poor senses, yet I was playing against thousands. So far, I had beaten them all hollow. Every night that I closed my eyes, if I couldn't say — "Here's another honest day's work finished." — at least I could say: "Here's another day that I've beaten the whole world."

That was a pretty sweet satisfaction. It was seasoning in my food; it took the place of company. It was simply everything.

I don't know how long that life could have lasted. I've talked to wise fellows, since that time, who have told me that sooner or later I was sure to go down. They point out all the other outlaws who have prospered for a time, and the way that they have fallen. I have this to remark to the wise ones — that the outlaws that we hear about falling are always the ones that were captured or killed, of course. The men of the law aren't half so partial to talking about the outlaws that managed to keep their skins safe. To say nothing of the hundreds of crimes that are committed with nobody knowing who did them.

Now and then, somebody is revealed who committed a crime twenty years ago, and has been committing them ever since. Usually these revelations come by accident. What I want to point out is that there I was, a fellow untrained in crime, without any companions to show me the ropes, but I went off there among the mountains and maintained myself and lived pretty well, and had a good time of it, in a lonely way. My real belief is that any fellow who has the nerve to keep away from too much company always will give the law a hard run for its money.

However, I came to the end of my mountain life and my loneliness.

It was the idea that Jake had put into my head when I last saw him. I told myself that I would be a fool to do it — and yet it was never out of my mind day and night — the temptation to return to the house where I was said to have committed a murder. I wanted to see again the bed I was sleeping in when Les Burns came in and woke me up. I wanted to see again the room where the dead man lay.

Most of all, I wanted to see Les Burns himself to tell him just what I thought of him for having sent his cowpunchers on my trail, so hastily, and nearly being the means of getting me shot full of lead.

These foolish reasons were enough to start me back from the high mountains toward the house. So I closed one strange chapter, and I opened another that was just a mite stranger.

# CHAPTER
# NINE

I came to the house of Les Burns. It had just stopped raining. I had been securely wrapped in the great slicker that I had taken from Jake, months before. When the rain stopped, I had only to shake back the slicker — and I was dry and comfortable. When I came in under the trees near the house, every stir of air was knocking down rattling showers of rain water, so I went with double care.

Gray Maggie worried me more than a little. She had seemed pretty contented with me, in spite of the hard work that I had given her, but when she came near her old home, her head began to go up. I could hear, repeatedly, the beginning of a whinny forming in her throat. But she was a wonderfully sensible creature. When I tied her to a tree in a little circular opening near the house and patted her nose, she seemed to understand that her business was to keep quiet, and she was cropping the grass patiently before I left her.

When I came in under the wall of the house, I hesitated for a while about the way that I should enter the place. Finally I decided that I would come back through the very window by which I had escaped. That window was the one that opened off Les Burns's own room. When I had located that by the low balcony that ran in front of it, I started to climb.

There was a drainage pipe that ran down from the eaves gutter, and, though it was a pretty big handful, I managed to get a grip on it. I hoisted myself up until I came to the balcony. After that, it was easy to swing myself around, and I stood as comfortable as you please, looking through the opened window, able to see and hear all that went on in the room.

There was not much to happen there, at first. There was only the man that I most wanted to see — Les Burns. He sat at his desk, writing, and, as I watched him, I tell you that I hated him with my whole heart. I hated him so much that I reached for the butt of my Colt, but I had sense enough to understand that there was no need for gun play. I made ready to slide in through the window when there was a tap at the door, and I barely had the time to duck down again when Burns called: "Come in!" An Oriental servant came in.

"It is Gypsy Ogden," said the Oriental.

I thought that Burns would hit the ceiling, he was so mad. The Oriental started to go, but Burns loosened up a bit and ran to the door.

"Tell the drunken pig to come up anyway," he ordered.

He walked over to the window and stood there with his hands in his pockets, cussing soft and steady to himself all the time. His face was a regular study. I wondered how much blacker he would have looked if he had known that I was standing there in touching distance of him?

Pretty soon a step came down the hall, and the door was opened by a tall, well-made cowpuncher with the weakest-looking face that I ever saw in my life. Just plain good-natured and good-for-nothing — the sort of a fellow that would do anything for you — as long as it wasn't any trouble.

He stood there by the door, with his hands in his pockets and his sombrero on the back of his head. He looked as if he'd fallen down and taken a roll in the mud, but mud didn't bother Gyp very much. He was about two thirds lit. He wavered a little, even with the wall to lean against.

As for Les Burns, he was almost too mad to talk at all. He just stammered for a minute, then he said: "You walk into my house with your hat on your head now? And you open my door without knocking, Ogden?"

Gypsy Ogden took off his hat and brushed at the mud that was on it with a foolish-looking grin. I remembered where I had heard the name before this. This was the cowpuncher that the foreman had complained about on the night that I was accused of murdering that Jarvis. Gyp was to be fired, if he came back drunk. Yet here he was on the ranch, still — and it looked as if he'd been under the weather most of that time, by the fishy whiteness of his face.

It was curious. Because Les Burns was the last person in the world that you would expect to have any sympathy for the weakness of another man. It warmed me a little to him, to think that he would keep on a helpless old drunk like Gypsy.

"Well, chief," said Gypsy, "I guess that you're going to make a scene out of it again." He gave a sigh.

"You worthless, useless, flabby, weak-livered, hopeless rat!" hissed Les Burns.

He brought the words out through his teeth — like he was poison mean.

"All right," said Gypsy Ogden, "you go ahead and get all of your talking done. I'd rather have it finished in a lump than spread out over a long time."

"Words don't hurt you, do they?" asked Les Burns, sneering at him.

"Not much, they don't," said Gyp. "Do they hurt a duck? Take it by and large, the tonnage of words that has been throwed at me lays over the tonnage that any other man has had throwed at him, I suppose."

"You're proud of it, maybe?" suggested Burns.

"Why, there has been enough steam wasted, cussing me, to build another one of them pyramids. But here I am, just the same as ever."

He laughed a sort of a silly, weak, good-natured laugh. You couldn't hate this fellow; you could only pity him.

Les Burns was so mad, though, that he walked up and down a time or two before he could say anything at all. Then he asked: "Now what do you want? But mind, whatever it is that you want, don't tell me that it's money."

A lost look came into the eyes of Ogden. He took out a package of brown papers, thumbed one of them off, and sifted some tobacco out of his sack. He rolled that cigarette plumb fast and easy with one hand, and you could see that there was something to him besides foolishness. By the cut of him, somehow, I put him down for a mighty fine cowpuncher — gone wrong with liquor.

"Why don't you talk?" cried Les Burns. "Is this just a little social call, maybe? You think I like you so well that I want you to drop in and call on me? What is it you want out of me?"

"You've just said that I'm not to talk about it," said Ogden with a twisted smile.

"It's money again, then?"

Ogden shifted his cigarette to a corner of his mouth; he shifted his eyes, too, and lighted his smoke without saying a word.

"Money, you hound. And the last time you swore that you would never ask me again."

You could see that this tongue lashing hurt Ogden, but he stuck to his ground.

"I dunno what else I'm gonna do," he said at last. "I sure hated to come here to you."

"You hated to come here," Burns scoffed. "Then why didn't you stay away? Are you too proud to work?"

"Sort of too shaky to work. I tried it yesterday. All I want is enough to get sobered up on."

"You've told me that a dozen times before."

"It's kind of hard to have to starve."

"I gave you five hundred less than two weeks ago. You swore that would be the last penny you would expect out of me," said Burns. "And here you are, already. Confound you, how can you expect me to have any respect for you?"

"I suppose that there ain't much reason for you to respect me," said Ogden.

"What you want is cash, and not respect, eh?"

"I suppose that you might say that," said Ogden. "I hate to put it that way."

"You hate to put it that way! What other way is there to put it, then?"

Ogden hung his head.

"All that I want is forty or fifty," he said. "It ain't much . . . to you. You're pretty near made of money, Mister Burns!"

Burns turned. There was a devil in his face, but something made him swallow his anger. He pulled out his wallet and began to count out bills.

"Here's forty dollars," he said finally. "Now, Ogden, I give you this money for a reason that you know well enough. I want you to swear that it's the last time that I'll ever have to see your face."

"Mister Burns," said Ogden, with his pale face lighting up, "of course I'll give you my word. Here's my hand on it."

"Your hands are too dirty for a clean man to touch," said Burns. "Take the money and get out!"

Ogden blinked — but he pocketed the money and backed through the door. I heard his long, unsteady step going down the hall.

Of course, it was all pretty clear. Ogden knew something about Burns that Les didn't want popping out. That was the reason that he had shelled out money before, and that was the reason that he didn't dare to refuse to shell out this night.

**192**

All of this was clear, and I would have given a good deal to have known just what it was that the drunken cowpuncher knew about his boss. At the same time, I couldn't afford to bother my head about the business of other people. I had too much of my own affairs on my shoulders.

I waited until Burns, after sashaying up and down the room, cussing to himself and stopping and stamping like a child, settled down at his table to writing once more. Then I slid through that window.

I didn't make any more noise than a ghost, but something seemed to tell Burns that danger was coming. He turned around quick in his chair, pulling a gun as he turned.

# CHAPTER
## TEN

I reached for my own gat when I saw him swinging in his chair, but Les Burns had me fairly covered before I more than got started. However, he didn't fire.

If you wonder what it was that saved me, I'll tell you. It was the editors that had been writing so many columns about Garver, the desperado. Here was Les Burns, with a good deal more than the courage of the average man, and a good deal straighter shooting and faster shooting than I could ever hope to brag of. But when he saw me, he just dropped the gun that covered me into his lap and gaped at me.

He would fight anybody that was his equal as quick as a wink. When it came to trying his hand with the great desperado, Garver, he simply wasn't equal to it at all. It froze up his blood and his courage, and he let the gun fall while I brought out my own Colt, feeling none too comfortable until I had a look at his face. It was simply whitewashed with fear.

I couldn't help saying: "Buck up, Les. I haven't come back to murder you."

He had to moisten his lips before he could speak at all.

194

Then he said: "How long have you been outside that window?"

It was plain that he didn't want me to have seen poor Ogden. Since what a man doesn't know doesn't hurt him any, there was no reason why I should tell, and I didn't.

"About ten seconds."

He gave a terrible big sigh of relief, and a shade of color came back into his cheeks. He said: "Well, Garver, the last time that you were in this house, I treated you like a skunk. I'm ready to apologize."

"You didn't give me much more than a sporting chance to get clear, Les," I said. "And I've held it pretty hard against you, I admit. Just the same, I think that I can understand. There was nobody in the house except you and me, and Jarvis. And if I wasn't blamed for the killing, why, maybe they would have dumped the blame all on you."

He shook his head.

"Never on me," he said. "What in the world would I have had to gain by the death of Jarvis?"

"Oh, I don't know," I said. "That Kate Mullen, for one thing, I suppose."

He jumped right out of his chair and glowered at me.

"What the devil do you mean by that?"

"Don't take it so hard," I said. "I'm willing to forget that night and what you did on that night, and the reasons why you did them. But I'll tell you what, old-timer. There's something else that I would like a lot to talk to you about."

"Fire away," he said. "Matter of fact that night lies on my conscience more than you'd suspect. I should have let you get clear away . . . but I got rattled when I reached the door and remembered the dead man lying in the room above, and nobody in the house to put the blame of the murder on. It was a low thing that I did. The lowest of my whole life. It's pretty white of you to be willing to overlook that."

It warmed me a good deal to him, hearing him talk like that. And a familiar face was a lot of comfort to me, after I'd been out wandering through the mountains all these weeks, dodging danger pretty regularly and living more lonely than a hermit.

I put up my Colt. That didn't seem to make any difference in the way that Les looked at me. The newspapers had done their work pretty well, and they had given me such a reputation that even a pretty well-educated fellow like Burns forgot his sense of humor when he sat there facing me.

He said: "Well, old-timer, I owe you a debt. And I wonder what I can do to pay it?"

"Burns," I replied, "you don't owe me a thing. But I'll admit that I've come here to ask you for help. It's nothing that you owe me, though, and it's nothing that you have to do. I'm not here to bulldoze you, and I'm not going to extract favors at the end of a Colt. I'm asking you, as an old friend, to give me a lift. But you can turn me down after you hear what it is."

"Old boy," said Burns, very hearty, "you step out and name what it might be, and I'll bet that I'll want to do it for you, no matter what it costs me."

"I can tell you pretty easy and quick. I've been hounded up and down the mountains for a long time. That sort of a life is well enough, but in the end I'm afraid that a man has got to eat lead, or else he's got to step into bigger crimes than any that I've ever committed. Ever committed knowingly, maybe I had ought to say."

I curled up a little inside, thinking about the other thing.

Burns threw a look over his shoulder.

"Don't go on about that," he said, soft but sharp. "Let it go, man. It was the liquor, and not yourself. It was done in your sleep. You couldn't help it."

I shook my head. The things that a man does when he's under the influence of alcohol simply *can't* be counted out. Not to himself at least.

I went on. "I've tried that lonely life, and I like it pretty well, I have to admit. I like it so well that I'm afraid of myself. I want to do something besides become a gunfighter the rest of my days. As a matter of fact, I want to break away from the country, and I'll tell you what my scheme is, if you'll listen."

"Never gladder to listen to anything," said Burns. "Blaze away and go the limit."

"I want to work to the sea coast, and, when I get to the coast of Mexico, say, I want to get aboard of some tramp freighter that's bound for the Pacific Islands, or some such place. When I get there, I want to be wearing a new name and be ready to step out with a new life, if you know what I mean. I'm young still. But I'm fairly old to be making a start. I want to make that start soon, or it'll be too late. Now, old-timer, I can go across country, working my way with my gun . . . and hunted all the time. Or else I can go across country wearing a little hard cash in my pocket. It's on account of the hard cash that I've come looking for you."

He nodded at me, very friendly, and said: "I'm with you every minute. What do you think that you'll need?"

"About three or four hundred will do it," I said.

"All right," said Les Burns. "We'll call that five hundred, and make it a go at that. Wait here for a minute while I slip downstairs and get it out of the safe. I don't wear that much money in my buttonhole every day of my life."

He got up and walked out of the room. At the door, he turned and said: "I'll be only a minute, as soon as I get the combination of that rusty old box working."

Then he went down the hall, and I sat there, a little bit nervous.

This Burns sounded right and talked right and acted right. Just the same, I couldn't help remembering some important facts. One was that the first time I met him I got to know him by dumping him on his back, taking the football away from him, and beating his team with the touchdown that came afterwards. The second time I met up with him, I ran away from his house with a lot of cowpunchers aching to get my hide, with their six-guns in their hands.

Two starts like that didn't point to any happy little road lying ahead of us, as you can see for yourself. So, after I had been sitting there for a minute, I couldn't help jumping up.

I opened the door of the room into the hall, moving the latch very soft and careful and I sneaked down to the stairs, stopping at the first landing because I could hear a voice down on the first floor. It sounded like Les Burns's.

No matter what a man may think of his money safe, he doesn't talk to it. So I slipped down those stairs for a little ways, and I heard Les Burns saying:

"There isn't time to explain anything more. That's the way that it stands. I'm going now to get the money that I promised him. When I give it to him, I'll try to delay him with a little talk. You ought to be able to get here in five or ten minutes with your men, and, if you do, you'll have a prize. Man, don't ask any more questions, but hop onto your horses with your men, and come here tearing all the way."

That was what I got for taking the lessons from grizzly bears and taking nothing for granted. My fine friend, Les Burns, was crooking me again and double-crossing me pretty bad. I up and went back up the stairs and sat down in his room and waited for him.

Maybe you'll wonder why I waited. As a matter of fact, I wanted that money, and the plan that I'd broached to him was still the plan that I intended to follow. I hadn't very long to wait.

Pretty soon a quick step came down the hall, and the door opened. There was Les Burns, as cheerful and gay as you please. With one hand he pressed the money on me. With the other hand, he grabbed my arm and gave it a good, firm, friendly grip.

"I wish you the best of luck in the whole world, old-timer," he said, "but there's no rush about going. I want you to stay here a minute and talk to me a little while. Most of all, I want to look you over. You've changed, Garver. I wouldn't believe some of the reports that I've been reading about you in the papers, but now I see that they're true, and maybe less than the truth. You have a real wild look, old boy."

"I'll tell you what's given it to me," I said as I shoved the money away. "It's old friends that have pretended to stick by me, and that have double-crossed me like dirty dogs."

He went back a long step from me as though I had hit him in the face.

# CHAPTER
# ELEVEN

What I should have done, of course, was to take the money that he had brought me; with that money I should have started out of the country, just as I had planned. That was, of course, the logical and the reasonable thing for me to do. Somehow, to rob Les Burns of the money would have seemed to me a better and a squarer thing than to let him give it to me, and pretend that I thought he was a friend, and not let him know that I saw through him, at the last. He looked at first as though he was afraid that I was going to murder him.

I only said: "Why did you have to do it, Les? What the devil good is it going to do you to have me dead? Won't I be out of the way when I'm in China, or wherever it was that I could have gone? What good is it to you for me to be in a coffin? Are you hankering after the price that they've put on my head?"

Les Burns didn't flush. He didn't do anything but just look at me, and into his eyes he couldn't put a lie. The truth came there for a glimmering minute and gave me a good look at such hate and malice as I never have seen before in the eyes of any man.

He wanted me dead. There was no doubt about that. It would please him a lot to see the finish of me. And it would please him a lot if he could sit in and see the end.

Why should he hate me so?

I hadn't much time. Somewhere on the road toward his house there were men riding hard and fast for the sake of nailing me. But for the lucky chance that I had followed this dog part way and overheard him, they would have caught me dead to rights sitting there, in Burns's own room and acting very proud of myself. I couldn't waste many minutes, but still I was fairly bulging with curiosity to learn why it was that Burns had done such a low thing.

"Les," I said, "if you tell me the truth, I'll go and leave you safe. Just the truth . . . no matter what it may be. Tell me the truth, Les, and I'll leave you without harming you none. What makes you hate me so bad? Tell me true . . . is it just because I helped to beat the Whitman team that you was captain of, all of those years ago?"

He hung his head. I couldn't tell whether it was in shame or else to hide the glitter of his eyes.

"That was the starting of it, Garver. I'm ashamed. But shame doesn't do you any good."

"Telling you how low you are," I said to Les Burns, "won't do any good. All that a dog like you lives for is to keep fooling the other people. When you're alone with yourself, you've got no peace of mind. You don't dare to think about yourself and what you are. Because you know that you're a liar and a faker. You know it and

202

you pretty near despise yourself. But what I have to tell you now, old-timer, is just this . . . you may fool the folks part of the time, but finally they'll see right through you, and they won't have to listen to you talking on the telephone to do it. The truth about a sneak like you is something that ripens and ripens, but finally the time comes when it's got to be known. Les, I suppose that, by rights, if I was to do justice on you, I'd do the world a good turn by blowing the top of your head off, but I'm not going to touch you. All that I'm gonna do is to leave you here, knowing that you're a skunk, and that I wouldn't take a penny of your dirty money. Wait a minute. Here's the change from what I took before."

I had used his $200 pretty sparingly while I was going up and down through the mountains. Now and then I would come to some pretty mean fellow, like Jake and his Maria. What I took from them had to be their gift. When I met up with a decent man, that meant right and wanted to see me have at least a sporting chance for my life, I saw to it that everything that he gave me was paid for a little more than in full.

That way, I had spent about $90, or a little more — which goes to prove to you that there wasn't such a terrible lot of mean folks in those mountains. Most of them were white men, and don't you make no mistake about it.

The change was more than half of what Les Burns had given me, as you may remember, on the night of the murder. I chucked that money with a good deal of satisfaction into his face, saying to him: "There's a part of your stuff. I'll find enough to make up the rest if I have to rob widows and orphans to get hold of it. You understand? Because to feel that you ever helped me to so much as a meal . . . is poison to me, Burns."

He stood through all of this with his head fallen and his eyes pretty low. Somehow I got the idea that he wasn't really ashamed of the position that he found himself in. I got a feeling that he was simply anxious to wait for me to get clear of the house, without showing any more of his natural meanness and lowness to me. He was glad of just one thing — that I was going to leave without sinking a bullet through his head.

However, I had told him what I had intended to do, and I had told him that he was safe. I wouldn't change my mind now. Only — what a terrible temptation it was to stand there in reach of him and not hit him just one solid punch.

I climbed back through the window — keeping my eyes on him all the time — and so down to the ground. I got back to Gray Maggie in the shrubbery, and was rubbing the softness of her nose, while I thanked heaven for an honest horse, at least — when I heard a pounding of horses' hoofs die out down the road, and then a softer sound of men hurrying along on foot. Those fellows who were coming for me had somebody at their head who knew his business pretty well. He wasn't taking any chance of scaring me out with the noise of a cavalry charge.

Getting on Gray Maggie, I eased her through the trees to the edge of them, from where I could see what approached the house from the road.

204

For a minute I thought there was a whole army coming. It seemed to me that I could count thirty, with the first sweep of my eye. I guess maybe that was too much. Anyway, there was a full twenty. That was a pretty thickly settled strip of country — there between the mountains where the valley bottoms were so rich. I looked these fellows over, and I knew what a good turn my old friend, Les Burns, had intended doing for me. These boys all meant business. They all carried rifles, and there was something about them that told me that, if they ever got well started on my trail, they would make things tolerably hot for me.

That Gray Maggie was a regular cat, when it came to sneaking through brush. The last months, she had had a good deal of practice with me, lying around here and there, stealing up on a shack in the mountains, and then stealing down again. I took her down the side of the trees until I came to a lot of shadows against the stars that were on the horizon. When I came still closer, I could see that there was a knot of about twenty-five or thirty horses all gathered right at the side of the road.

They were gathered into three bunches, and I saw that each of the three bunches had one man in the center of it, holding the reins of the bridles. Three pretty flowers they made, with every petal made up of a fine horse and its saddle, and the center of each of those three flowers was a cowpuncher that I intended to turn into a sucker, if I could, in about another minute.

I worked Gray Maggie along until she was lying mighty close to the first bunch. Then I climbed into the saddle, and hung from it Indian style, with one leg hooked behind that saddle and my body down low along the body of the mare. In that way, unless the starlight should wink on my spur, I was pretty sure of being able to sneak in among the horses without being discovered.

It worked fine. Only, when I began to jam Gray Maggie into that first knot of eight or ten nags, the chap who was holding the reins began to cuss his horses for huddling around and fussing, the way that they were doing. Then he saw Gray Maggie, farther back than the rest.

He said: "I've dropped one pair of the reins. Steady, old hoss. Steady, cutey. Steady, baby."

He came easing himself along, slow and careful and talking baby talk that would make you laugh to hear it. I hated to do it; I sure hated like sixty to do it. But here I was with a chance to cut the ground away from under the twenty-five or thirty good men and true that were ready to hound the life out of me at the house of Les Burns.

I had to swallow my feeling of friendship for this poor devil; I had my revolver butt ready to tap him on the head at the first, but when I decided that he was a pretty good sort, I changed my mind. I slid that Colt back into its holster, braced myself, and slugged that chap with my bare fist. I only had starlight for the work, but that punch landed fair and square. The big boy curled up and sat down like a tame cat on the hearth. He only let out one grunt.

One of his pals sang out: "Hello, Roscoe! What's up? How's things?"

Before he could answer, those horses that he had been holding reared back from him. He dropped the reins. As they swung around, ready to bolt, I fired a shot into the air, gave a yell, and swung up into my saddle, waving my hands.

It was so easy that there wasn't anything to it. Most of those horses were mustangs, and the others could take a bad example as well as the next one. In ten seconds, there were two dozen horses tearing down that road. There were three cowpunchers, lying flat in the dust, groaning. How badly they had been hurt by the stampede, I didn't stop to ask any questions about. I just lit out behind that flock of horses to help them along. The farther they ran their heads off, the longer it would be before the gents back at the house of Les Burns would be able to chase me.

# CHAPTER
# TWELVE

Take it all in all, that little play had turned out as well as anybody could expect, and I was pleased with myself. Here were three of the sheriff's boys laid out so that they wouldn't want to do any riding or manhunting for a long time, and here were the horses of the rest of the posse clean gone. Maybe the last of them wouldn't be gathered again for days and days.

I followed along in the rear of that mob of horses for a time. As soon as I was out of the sight of the three men who were groaning in the road, I cut back across country, and put Gray Maggie in close to the house of Les Burns. I got there in time to hear the boys down the road firing signals that they needed help, and needed it badly. The whole swarm came out from the house. They were cussing mad, and they fairly burned up the air with what they had to say about me. Les Burns came in for his share of the talk, too, for bringing them over here on a wild-goose chase. Then they walked off down the road with their spurs *jingling*.

While I was still sitting in the saddle in the trees, watching and laughing, Les Burns came out, got on his own horse, and rode off in a different direction down the road. I followed him — not because I was particularly curious about where he was going, but because I didn't know what better there was to do, and time was pretty free on my hands.

He rode for about two miles and a half. Then he turned in at a lane just beside a little wayside saloon. The lane wound up to a small house back in the woods. I cached Gray Maggie away and sneaked up close.

When I got within earshot, there was my friend, Les Burns, sitting on the front porch with an old man and a girl. Burns was telling a long lie — about one of the most able-bodied lies that I ever had the pleasure of listening to. He said as how he had been sitting in his house, not thinking any harm, when in pops Garver, the outlaw, and takes a shot at him. The shot just missed his head, and he put up his hands — not having his own gun handy. Then Garver changed his mind about murdering him and just decided to rob him. He took $1,500 in hard cash that was on Burns.

But Garver forgot that there was a telephone in the place, and Burns managed to get away for a single minute to telephone for help. Then he went back and tried to keep Garver in conversation until the posse and the sheriff should have arrived. Though he almost succeeded, Garver was too suspicious.

He left at the last minute, just before the sheriff and the sheriff's men came. Then Garver rode down the road and shot down the three men that were watching the horses, and stampeded them all. The three men were left there, very badly hurt.

That was the main outline of the lies that Les Burns told — but only the skeleton. The way he embroidered that little yarn was pretty good to listen to. He described me in a way that sounded like I was a natural-born murderer and ruffian. The lust for killing was in my eyes, said Les Burns. Everything else that he told about me was fetched just as big and broad as that.

The two on the porch swallowed about everything that he had to say, for a time, until finally the girl spoke up in a voice that did me good to hear.

"I don't think that most of these desperadoes are any different from other men," said the girl. "I saw Billy McElvey when he was riding up and down the country with his killings, and Billy was simply a badly frightened young boy. That was all there was to him. He was afraid of being caught, and he was so badly afraid that he always had his guns ready, and he was always ready to kill. That was the trouble with Billy. He was simply too high-strung and too nervous. He started in by running away, because he hadn't the money to pay a little ten-dollar debt that he owed. That grew into eleven killings, before he finished. But that's usually the way. It's the *running away* that does the harm. It really is. Once they begin to run, they begin to commit crimes. Consider this poor fellow, Garver . . ."

"Are you gonna start pitying *him*, Kate?" asked the old man.

"I do pity him, Father," said Kate.

"You can trust Kate for that," said Les Burns. "She will always pick up for the underdog, Mister Mullen."

This name gave me a good deal of a shock. Mullen was the last name, and Kate was the front name of the girl that had been engaged to marry that faker and

**210**

bluffer, Jarvis. You may remember how I had seen her picture in the watch case of that bounder? I listened with a lot more interest.

What was Les Burns doing up here?

"You may laugh at me," said Kate Mullen, "but I do wish that I could send a message to poor Garver. He's riding up and down the mountains, acting a great deal like a hero and a good deal like a fool, because, sooner or later, he will have to fight, and, when he fights, he will have to kill. You say that he shot down three men tonight. Maybe that's the beginning of the end of Garver. His nerves have been strong enough to keep him from shooting before this. It's when their nerves begin to fail them that they distrust what the other fellow may do, and then they shoot, and shoot to kill. But Garver ought to be saved, Les. I don't care how bitterly you feel about him, after he killed a man in your house. There's something mighty decent about Garver."

"*Bah*, Kate, you're talking plumb foolish!" exclaimed her father.

Les Burns laughed, very sarcastic.

"I'm a mite near-sighted about that, I admit," he said. "After you've seen a man shot through the head while lying in bed in your own house . . ."

"It was whiskey that did that, rather than Garver's own wish. You know it, Les. If he had been the sort of a red-handed killer that you're making him out now, he *would* have killed you, too, before he left. But you found him asleep in his room after the killing. That's your own story."

"Because he never dreamed that the killing would be traced home to him so quickly," said Les Burns, a little snappy. "When I cornered him and made him confess, he nearly broke down. He would have killed me, then and there, except that Garver is afraid of me. I don't know why it is. Except that I used to play football against him in the old days. I could beat him, then, and I imagine that he's never forgotten some of the lessons that I gave him on the football field, you see."

That was smooth talk. He lied with a sort of an easy grace, that Les Burns did. It made me hot. It would have made anybody hot. I had the sense to lie quiet and do nothing and say nothing, though I wanted nothing so much as to have a chance at Les Burns right then and there, before the two of them, and show them how badly he had lied, and how much he was the master of me, even without guns at all in the argument.

That was the way I was feeling when the old chap, Mullen, yawned and said that he would go to bed. He leaned for a minute against one of the wooden pillars of the porch.

"You must come over soon to supper, Les," he said. "Since we're gonna have you in the family so soon, we may as well start in to get used to you, I suppose."

That gave me another wriggle. Les Burns was to marry this decent girl, then? It made me hotter and hotter. I can't tell what a liking I had taken for her. You may remember that back in the beginning, when I first saw her picture, she had looked like the real thing, and I had wondered how come she could have picked out a pill like that Jarvis for a man to marry.

Now that Jarvis was a dead man — by my hand, as they said — what was to hinder her from finding somebody that was *real?*

She had turned around and found the only person on the map that was just as bad as Jarvis, or maybe worse. What she had picked out was this lying, faking, four-flushing piker, Les Burns!

Some girls are like that. They've got all the sense in the world until it comes to men. Men they can't pick out at all. Sometimes it seems as though the finer and the better that a woman is, the lower percentage of chances there is that she'll pick out the right man. Otherwise, the world would very soon be different. If the good women married the good men, there would soon be just two classes — good folks and bad folks. That would be all that there could be to it.

Girls like poor Kate seemed to be the ones that kept things from getting in this fix. They give a chance to those of us that ain't up to the scratch. They make us wives so nice that people will receive us just for the sake of the girls that we have married.

Anyway, there I crouched in the night and hated that Les Burns with my whole heart. The old man, Mullen, went inside the house, and there were the lovers, left to spoon on the porch. I was pretty sick, and I got ready to sneak away. What I heard made me stop.

"If I were Garver," said Kate Mullen, "I'd certainly go in now and surrender myself."

"And get yourself hanged?" asked Burns, laughing. "No, Garver is not that kind of a fool."

"I'm perfectly serious. I'd go in and surrender myself, and I'd take what was coming to me. In the first place, it wouldn't be hanging."

"Why not?"

"Because Garver is too popular, for one thing. And for another, he only has to stand up and tell a judge and a jury the same queer story that he told you. About not really knowing what he had done. And they would believe him."

"Never!"

"Ah, but they would. Because he's proved that he's no professional killer. He's proved that in the time that he has been wandering up and down the range, with a thousand temptations to kill right and left. And the people believe in him. I tell you that women and children would trust themselves to Garver, Les."

Les Burns swore loud enough for me to hear, and then he apologized very profusely, but his voice was shaking with anger.

"Well," he said, "I didn't come here to ask you about your opinions of Garver. I came to tell you he had just finished trying to murder me."

"Les, now that we are alone, do you mean to tell me that Garver really fired at you when your back was turned on him? Will you look me in the eye and tell me that?"

Bless her, she fair staggered me by the way that she was standing up to him for the sake of a stranger that she had never seen in her life.

It staggered Les Burns, too. Good liar that he was, he couldn't very well outface her in a case like this. He hesitated just a second or two, and then he busted out: "Kate, do you accuse me of lying to you?"

"Come," said Kate Mullen, very dry, "don't pose for a saint, Les, because you're not one. Let's be frank and honest with one another, please, because I tell you frankly that that's the only way that I can ever get along with you, or you with me. There's only one way to run a marriage that's a loveless affair ... that's by open-eyed partnership and friendship, Les."

"If you hate me as much as all this, Kate ... ?" he cried.

"I don't hate you," said Kate. "And you're acting a good deal like a sulky child. You know the truth about this, Les. I don't hate you. I know what you've done for my father. Just the way that ..."

"I know ... Jarvis. Don't class me with Jarvis again. I've heard you do it too often before."

She said nothing.

"Well," said Les, beginning to pace up and down the porch, "this is sweet, this is. A fine way we are getting on together."

Still she said nothing. It might be that he was taking a good deal from him for the sake of her father, but she wouldn't cringe to him. I cursed Les Burns with my whole heart, and then and there I swore that I would never let Kate Mullen throw herself away on a cur like Burns.

"Ah, Kate," Les said at last, "I can't live without you and you know it, and you take advantage of me to ..."

"Hush," said Kate. "I don't think that we'd better talk very much longer this evening. I'm going to ask you to leave me alone, Les. For tonight. Will you say good bye and shake hands in a friendly way? I'll see you again tomorrow, whenever you choose to come over."

He chose to do what she told him to do, without too much argument. He showed a pile of good sense in that, because there was a lot of iron strength in the voice of the girl, let me tell you.

"All right," said Les Burns. "I'm going. And as for this Garver . . ."

He didn't finish that sentence, but went hurrying off down the path, mounted his horse, and rode off like mad, quirting the poor beast with every stride that it took. It was plain that he was taking out all his anger on the horse.

When I stepped out into the shadows, I was in half a mind to ride Gray Maggie after him, take him down in the dust of the road, and tell him what he was worth and what he amounted to. But whether I had to kill him or not, I knew that I should prevent that marriage of Kate Mullen and Les Burns.

# CHAPTER
# THIRTEEN

I sent Gray Maggie winding down the lane to the road, and I passed a reeling figure. It was Gypsy Ogden wavering down the road.

What mischief he had been up to, I didn't know, but I knew that he was not too far gone with liquor to respond when I rode up to him and jammed a gun under his chin.

He straightened with a yell that stopped as it begun. "What's wrong? What have I done?"

"Kid," I said, "do you know me?"

He looked at me hard, standing perfectly straight and without any wobbling about — he'd been sobered so thoroughly by the sight of my Colt and the cold feel of its nose in his neck. There was a thin bit of a moon showing over the edge of the eastern mountains, and, altogether, there was light enough to see trouble, if you know what I mean by that. When he studied me, it didn't seem to mean much to him, but when he got a good look at Gray Maggie, he sort of wilted.

"It's Garver!"

I thought that he would slide down into the road.

"Buck up," I said. "You aren't dead yet. And maybe you won't die if you keep your head about you and tell me what I want to know."

"Garver," he said, "I ain't any hero. I ain't got any intention of trying to get famous on you. Will you please point that gat another way?"

"Sure," I agreed, "if you can stay sober without me using the Colt by way of an ice pack."

I even dropped the Colt into the holster. It was a mistake. But you've had a chance to hear what sort of a gent this here Gypsy Ogden was, and I think you would agree that it was surprising to see the play that he attempted now. The minute that my gun was up, he leaped at me like a wildcat and tried to pull me off my horse.

He came at me so fast that I didn't have a chance to parry. He let me have a punch as I fell, but it glanced off the side of my skull, down my cheek, and didn't do much more than shock the wits back into my brains again.

I fell on top of that lanky, lean Gypsy Ogden. I had a shade of advantage in weight on him, and certainly every advantage in training and condition. Trying to get hold of him was like grasping a snake; he pretty nearly wriggled out from my grip before his bad condition told on him. Then he went limp in one gasp, and told me that if I didn't get off of him, he would die for the lack of air.

I kind of believed him, too. I doused half the water in my canteen into his face, and then I took him by the nape of the neck and sat him up against a tree. He was as limp as a rag, and he sat there with his head fallen back and his arms hanging very weak at his sides.

"All right, Gypsy," I said, "you're poison, and you pretty near got me down. If you'd had a chance to get out my gun from that holster, you would have been pretty prosperous, before tomorrow night, I guess?"

He sat silent for a minute, turning things over in his mind.

"No," he said. "I've got pretty low, but I don't think that I would have turned you in. Not after you put up your gun when I asked you to. That was a fool play that you made there, though."

"Gyp, you're about a hundred times as much of a man as I thought that you were."

"If I ever get sobered up for ten days," said Gypsy, "I'm gonna show a dozen or so folks around here that they're wronger than you. Well, Garver, what do you want of me?"

Pretty cool, that. Pretty cool from a kid like that, lying on the flat of his back against a tree, helpless, after having tried to knock my head off.

"Why," I said, "I'm just turning things over in my head. And I dunno whether or not I had ought to fix you for trying to double-cross me. I dunno whether I hadn't ought to put a bullet through your head, kid."

Gypsy just lay back there and laughed at me, very weak. He was an amazing kid.

He said: "Oh, no, Garver, you ain't gonna do anything like that."

"You think that I'm tired of killings?"

"Old-timer," asked the kid, "did you ever take a shot at a man in your whole life?"

It called the turn, all right. I never had. But it made me sort of mad to hear a young pup like that talking back to me so confident and free. Being looked up to and sort of reverenced all the time that I was running wild had spoiled me, as you might say.

"You young rat," I said, "you take it for granted that I won't do you no harm, do you?"

"Look here, Garver, if I hadn't known that you were no killer, d'you think that I would have taken a free punch at you?"

I laid a hand on my cheek. It was swelling badly, where that kid had soaked me. It made me madder and madder.

"I got a mind to tie you to that tree and leave you there until the morning with a gag between your teeth," I said.

"No, you won't. You're too dog-goned law abiding even to do a thing like that."

Darned if he didn't loll back his head and begin to laugh again, very hearty and free and easy.

"You take a lot of liberties with a gent that does murders while folks are stretched on their beds asleep," I said.

"Murder them in their beds? Say, Garver, d'you think that I don't know the facts?"

"What facts?" I asked.

He shut up tight and seemed to feel that he had talked a little too free.

"All right," he said. "I've said enough."

"You've only started," I said. "You're going to spout a whole lot more."

"Not a word," he replied.

"Kid," I said, "don't make any mistakes. I won't do anything that'll endanger your life. But I'll certainly take a pass at you, if you won't tell me what you know. I would tie you back there in the woods and quirt you within an inch of you life, young feller. Because the idea is beginning to dawn in my head that *I didn't kill Jarvis, after all*."

To tell you the truth, it was just at that moment that the happy idea came home to me.

The kid sat up and gaped at me. "Why, you poor, hypnotized fish," he said, "did you ever think that you did?"

That knocked the ground right out from under my feet.

"Tell it to me easy, Gypsy," I coaxed, "because it's plain that you can't keep on pulling money out of Les Burns much longer. He's getting too sore at you."

The kid stood right up before me.

"Look here," he said, "how comes it that a bonehead like you has been able to find out that Les Burns was paying me any money?"

"Forty or fifty dollars isn't much," I answered, "but it's something. It's enough for one party . . . even if it isn't enough to get sobered up on."

He saw that I had overheard his talk with Burns that same night, and it seemed to make a pretty deep impression on him.

"Now," I said, "will you talk to me?"

"Take it all around," he exclaimed, "this here is a sweet mess!"

"Will you talk, or do I get the quirt?"

"Take it easy," said the kid. "You don't bluff me. Not tonight. I'm so low, old-timer, that the little matter of getting a horsewhipping don't shame me none . . . and as for the pain, I wouldn't feel it."

"You don't know the kind of a quirt that I use, if you think that way, my son."

"Aw," said the kid, "I would faint after the first couple of cuts, and then you could whale along as far as you liked. It wouldn't make no difference to me."

You couldn't beat that Gypsy Ogden. He was just different from other folks. I stood back and wondered at him, I can tell you. He was a surprise in every way that you took him. All that you first could see in him was weakness and lowness, but, when you looked closer, you could see very easily that there was a lot of real manliness in him. He was weak with booze, but his muscles were strong by nature. He was fast enough to tag a lightning flash and get back to his corner of the ring before the bolt had struck the floor. He was handsome, too, and that long, well-built fighting jaw hadn't been given to him for nothing. No, he was a wreck, and a young wreck, and I couldn't help wondering why it was that somebody couldn't salvage that kid and save him from himself.

"All right, Gyp," I said, "I take your word for it, and you have me beat. You talk if you want to, or you keep silent if you want to. I can't handle you."

The kid busted into laughter once more. "You are easy. Why, bonehead, do you think that I would let you touch a whip to me? Not without killing you or dying in the try. However, you have something coming to you. You have a lot coming to you from me, and right here is where you get it all back. Just tie yourself together and do a little listening."

# CHAPTER
# FOURTEEN

The moon was wiped out by an arm of clouds, and the same arm began to travel across the sky while he was talking. Off in the trees, in the distance, we could hear the wind moaning and rushing a long time before it ever came to us.

Gypsy Ogden said to me: "Look here, partner, if I go back to the beginning, I got to tell you that I'm a mean and slimy low one. But you know that. You've seen me stand up and beg from Les Burns and take the talk of that rat, like I liked it. So you know how low I am. But I was never a fool ... except about the booze, y'understand?"

I nodded.

"But to get right down to action ... on the night that Jarvis was murdered in his bed ..."

"He was murdered, then?" I asked, feeling a hope slide away from me.

"Didn't you see him?"

"Yes ... but suicide ..."

"You think that a fathead like Jarvis could ever get anything on his conscience enough to make him shoot himself? Think again, old-timer, because you're all wrong!"

Seeing that I was, I began to get more and more excited.

He went on: "When I came back to the house that night, I had promised to be home by suppertime, and here it was pretty late. I was feeling a little restless, because the foreman was already pretty much off on me. When I came by the big house, I saw the flash of a light in the lower hall, and I went up on the front porch softly, because it occurred to me that it was pretty late for anybody to be roaming around at that time of the night.

"I got on the front porch and peeked through the curtains, and there I seen the big boss . . . I mean, Les Burns . . . sneaking along with a lamp in his one hand and a Colt in the other."

I broke in: "Man, what are you driving at?"

"Limber up your vocabulary, old man," said the kid, "because you'll need everything you got to express yourself in a minute. I thought that the way Burns walked wasn't the way that an honest man walks.

"Just then, my foot slipped, and I made a little noise on the verandah. Not much of a noise at all, but it was enough to get to the ear of Burns. He gave a twitch around and looked at the window where I was standing in the night. There was murder broad and plain wrote on his face, as ever I seen it before. Believe you me, I've seen it before.

"I decided that I would have to see something more of what he was going to do. I couldn't enter the house and watch him, so I climbed up to the second story, along the balcony that stretched there. I came outside of a room where there was a light burning inside of the window, and there I looked in on this piker, Jarvis, stretched out in the bed reading a magazine, yawning at it to beat the band. Probably it was wrote too good for Jarvis, y'understand?

"I just about had time to see that, when the door of the room opened soft and slow, and there was Les Burns, standing, with his eyes as green as a cat's. He let in a draft, and big Jarvis turned his head to watch the flame leap in the throat of the lamp chimney beside his head. When that happened, Les Burns took a long step forward, almost laid his Colt beside the head of Jarvis, and fired.

"Jarvis gave a sort of groan and yell, combined. He tumbled out on the floor, all twisted in the bedclothes, and lay there on his back, with his arms thrown up above his head. And there you are, old-timer."

I put a hand against the trunk of the tree and leaned there, dizzy, sick, and terribly happy. I never knew before what happiness could be. Thousands of tons were sliding off the shoulders of my soul and breaking away in chunks, leaving me so light that I could have jumped up and caught the moon right out of the sky. You understand? I was no murderer, after all. My hands were clean.

"I was about to break in and face Les Burns . . . I always hated him," said the kid, "but when I reached for my Colt, I found that I didn't have one. Right then and there, I swore that I'd never carry one again, if I lived to be a hundred. Because I didn't have it with me the one time when it was my right to do a killing.

"I went on back to the bunkhouse, and, when I got there, the liquor was working in me again. I went to sleep. The next day . . . why, the next day I didn't have the nerve to go tell the sheriff what the sheriff ought to know. I didn't have the nerve, and I'm ashamed of it. Besides, when I heard that you was off having your party through the mountains, it tickled me. I used to laugh when the folks told about the wild things that you was doing, and never pulling your Colt, at all. Because I knew that you weren't a killer . . . that you hadn't been one, and that you never would be."

That was the story that the kid had not told, all the time that I was wandering up and down the mountains, in danger of killing somebody or of being killed.

"Now, Gyp," I said suddenly, "you know pretty well that you would never tell this story on account of me. I don't mean a thing to you, and as for a conscience . . . why, you haven't got one. So please tell me what's made you confess this whole yarn to me tonight?"

"Why, I'll tell you that you're right. You didn't mean a thing to me when I first met up with you, but I like honest folks so long as they're really simple, y'understand? And I really want to do you a good turn now, Garver. The main reason is something else . . . you're right. This rat, this Burns, killed Jarvis because maybe he owed Jarvis some money, or something like that, I thought at the time. But just the other day I found out the real facts . . ."

"He killed him because of a girl," I put in.

The kid started. "Why, you talk like you really knew something!" he gasped.

"And I *do* know something," I said. "I know enough to understand why you won't let him marry the girl. You'll talk the whole thing out to the sheriff before that happens?"

"Yes," said Gypsy Ogden, "I certainly will."

Here I was thinking that I would be playing the part of a regular hero by saving the girl from the villain, and all that, but I was only fooling myself. Quite apart from me, young Gyp Ogden would have taken her out of trouble and put the head of her lover into the hangman's noose. I had a sort of a liking for him before that, but, when I heard him say this, I really liked him a lot. He was decent — if you could only mine far enough beneath the surface to come to the decency. It was a streak of pay dirt, as you might say, that was out of sight.

When we had got to this point in our talk, I said to Gyp Ogden: "Gypsy, I think that I would sort of like to shake hands with you, you good-for-nothing 'puncher."

"Garver," said Gypsy Ogden, "I would like to shake hands with you, because you're honest."

We shook hands and stood there, grinning at each other like a pair of fools while the wind that had been whining and howling off there in the distance came again, washed a torrent of rain around us, and drowned out our voices with its roaring.

I was snug in one jerk at my slicker, and, when it was over my shoulders, I looked down at poor Gypsy, shuddering in the rain. I asked him if he would take my blanket, and we wrapped that around him.

"Well," I asked, "is the sheriff of this county young or old?"

"The sheriff don't know whether he's young or old," said young Gyp Ogden. "He's lying in bed with a bullet through him, fighting for his life. But the gent that runs things is a deputy that lives close by here."

"We'll give him a call," I said, "or is he still out chasing me . . . or his horses?"

"This rain will send him home."

We went down the road, and, in about thirty minutes, we were at a little quiet shack at the edge of some woods. A big-voiced dog started barking at us from the dark, and pretty soon a man hollered from the shack.

"Who's there?"

I sang out: "It's Garver!"

"You lie!" yelled the deputy sheriff. "This is a poor night to try that joke on me. Who are you, before I turn this dog loose to chaw you up?"

"I'm Garver," I said, "and I've come to give myself up, Sheriff."

"Matthews is his name," said Ogden. And then he piped up: "It's a lie, Matthews, I've brought him in . . . and he's under my gun!"

"Who are you?"

"I'm Ogden."

"Why, Gypsy Ogden, you hound . . . you ain't got the nerve to bring in a sparrow, let alone that devil, Garver. I'm gonna come out there, and, if I lay my hands on you jokers, I'll make things hot for you!"

He came with a lantern in one hand and a double-barreled, sawed-off shotgun in the other. When he came to us, he held up the lantern. I had passed my Colt to the kid, and what Matthews saw was me standing there with my hands up over my head, and a scowl on my face. There was Gypsy Ogden, looking cool and dangerous, with my own Colt jammed against my ribs.

"Take a look for yourself," said Gypsy. "This here ought to make me a respectable man again, Matthews."

Matthews couldn't speak for a minute. He could only stare. Then he jerked his gun to his shoulder.

"Garver," he said, "you're slick and you're smooth, but now I want to see you get yourself away from me."

"Matthews," I said, "I'll be a free man in five minutes. You leave it to me."

# CHAPTER
# FIFTEEN

I was a free man, well enough, though it took a little more than five minutes, while Matthews listened and swore, soft and deep. But finally I was free, and, before that hour was out, I was rapping at the door of the house of Les Burns.

It was lighted up, pretty well, on the inside. There was a lot of horses tethered outside the house — the boys of the posse had been chasing their horses, and they had finally fetched back a part of them, at least. Here they were on the inside, in Burns's dining room, having a bit of a party with Burns's liquor, making a little noise, and getting pretty happy.

Les himself opened the door and stepped back, singing out: "Come in and make yourself at home!"

I walked in right past him and stood there in front of them all in the blaze of light, with the water just sluicing down off of my wet slicker.

"Hey!" cried Burns. "Why don't you stop turning the hose on that carpet?"

Then he was attracted by the dead silence that had fallen around that table, and he walked around until he had a look at my face.

"Garver!" he cried, and he slung out a gun and covered me.

About a dozen others were doing the same thing. I never saw such a tonnage of guns flashing in my life, I give you my word.

"Stick up your hands!" cried Burns.

I put them up, willing enough, but I couldn't help smiling around at all those set, fighting faces, because I could see by the desperate look of them what they thought of me and my ways. They expected a miracle pretty near, but there was no miracle in me. I had lived in the middle of the world's grandest bluff for the past few months. Now I thought that there was no reason why I shouldn't give the boys one last thrill.

"Get around behind him . . . get between him and the door, some of you!" yelled Burns, shaking with excitement.

As some of them scrambled to do that, Burns said to me, white and savage with an ecstasy of revenge and hate: "Now, you murderer that takes men in their beds at night . . . now, Mister Garver, will you tell me how you're going to keep from jail tonight?"

"Old son," I said to him, "I'm not going to jail, if that will interest you any."

He blinked at me and sent a glance back at the window.

"Pile over there and guard those windows!" he screamed. "You fools, why are you standing there? Why don't you get out there and have a look to see whether or not he's got a gang there ready to tackle us when our backs are turned?"

There was no sense of humor in Burns. That was his fault.

His men got to the windows and jammed their heads and their guns out to look the landscape over.

"There's nothing here . . . it's all safe out here," said a couple of them.

"Then we've got you, and we've got you good!" cried Les Burns. "I've waited a long time, Garver, you swine, but I never thought that things would turn out as sweet as this!"

"Les," I said, "I'm sorry to see that you and the rest of the boys are as excited as all this, because I can't stay here with my hands in the air."

"Move those hands, and I drill you clean, Garver!" cried Les Burns. "Move those hands, and you're a dead man, Garver. I give you warning. I got witnesses here. If you move those hands, I'll have a cause for shooting . . . and I'll shoot quick, you murdering hound!"

You would have thought that he hated me for the good of society, that sneaking hypocrite.

"Another thing," I said, "you're not going to marry the girl, Les. The engagement is canceled."

I hit him where he lived; he turned a sickly white and glared at me.

"Curse you!" he exclaimed. "Do you think that you're still on a football field, where you can spoil my game?"

"Not a football field," I replied. "I don't need that sort of a field. I'll beat you at your own game, Les. You're beaten now, without knowing it, and, in another minute, you'll see me the freest man in this room."

I had them all pretty much excited by that time. They didn't know what to make of my coolness, and they were jerking their heads around and glancing back over their shoulders, to make sure that allies of mine didn't jump out of the solid walls around them.

"Grab him, half a dozen of you, and frisk him!" Les Burns ordered. "Take everything that he's got on him."

They jumped to do what he told them.

"Keep back!" I hollered at them. "Don't you lay a hand on me, boys."

They drew back.

"Do what I say!" yelled Les Burns.

"All right, boys!" I called.

The whole bunch stood frozen, waiting to see from what direction my gang would come. Then they heard the big, rough voice of Deputy Sheriff Matthews at the open door.

"Scatter, the whole lot of you. Les Burns, drop that gun!"

There was the long arm of the law reaching in among them, and they gave back in a terrible hurry — all but Les Burns. He saw the man of the law, but he couldn't see what was meant. He was staggered.

He could only say: "Matthews, Matthews, have you taken the side of this crook?"

"Steady," said Matthews. "Don't point that gun at me."

He came up and jerked the Colt out of the hand of Les Burns.

"You're very rough, Matthews," said Burns, scowling and dangerous. "What does it mean?"

"It means murder!" answered Matthews, who was not a very gentle man.

"Murder? Murder of whom?"

"Jarvis."

"Jarvis?" repeated Les Burns, and he rolled his eyes across at me. There was a silence in that room that weighed tons and tons — but not on me. I could stand there and grin, I tell you, because I had no sympathy for that Burns, and no pity for him. All he could get was not bad enough for him, so far as I could see.

He saw my smile, and it seemed to sicken him.

"Matthews," said Burns, "will you tell me in plain English just what this idiotic affair means? Because I want to know."

"It means," said Matthews, "that I arrest you for the murder of Jarvis."

It was a pretty horrible thing. You could see Burns jerk and quiver and go back a pace, just like a man hard hit in the ring.

"Who dares to accuse me of that?" asked Burns, his head sinking and a fighting scowl on his forehead.

"My friend, the kid," said the deputy sheriff.

He jerked his thumb over his shoulder toward Gypsy Ogden.

Gyp was rolling a cigarette, and smiling very gay and free.

"I'm sorry, old-timer," Gyp said to Burns. "I didn't want to do it. But I had to stop that marriage. A skunk like you don't rate a girl like Kate Mullen, you know. Besides, Garver turned out a white man. I would have had to do it even for his sake alone."

In the few seconds that he needed to finish that little speech of his, Les Burns saw that his finish had come. His mouth sagged open, and he licked his white lips. He began to pant, and his eyes jerked back and forth around the circle of faces where he had been the king, a moment before, but where he was worse than a rattlesnake, just now.

"Matthews," he muttered, "I want to explain, that I'm not going to die . . . alone . . ."

With that, he yanked out a Colt from inside his coat and took a snap shot at me.

I saw what was coming, but I slipped as I tried to dodge. I suppose that the slip saved me where the dodge wouldn't. I hit that floor an awful whack, but no bullet went through me. As I looked up from the floor, I saw Les Burns go down under the gun of the deputy sheriff.

He lived long enough to lie with his eyes closed, gasping out: "Thank heavens, I got him. I got him, first. Will some of you tell me where the bullet hit Garver?"

"Open your eyes and see for yourself," said the deputy sheriff.

Les Burns looked up with a start, and there he saw me, standing over him grinning — because I hated that man so thoroughly and completely that I couldn't pity him even when he lay dying.

"A miss!" gasped out Burns. "You swine, Garver."

He tried to shake his fist at me, and died in the act.

There are lots of ways to look at the crime of Burns — but it always seemed to me that it was the final of the football play out there on a high-school field, those many, many years ago. I had tackled Les Burns and made my run and my score — and here was Burns telling me what he thought of it with bullets.

He was a bad one, Burns — mighty bad, I'm sure.

As for me, well, there wasn't much to it. You see, there was a lot of folks that had scores against me, but when the judge heard my story, he advised the district attorney to drop the case, and the district attorney said that he had never wanted to bring it up, except for the sake of giving everything a thorough airing. That was where the matter dropped.

The only two people in the world that seemed to hold much against me were Jake and Maria. They were pretty peeved, but when I had paid them principal and interest for the things that I "borrowed" from them, even Jake and Maria seemed to cool down a lot, though they said that it was a terrible country where honest householders were not protected from roving bandits.

Which leads me to the last point of all. I've been a sober, steady, hard-working man the rest of my life. Yet even between my best friends, who know my story backwards, and me, there's still a barrier. They try to think that I'm honest, but they still feel in their hearts that I'm only Garver, the bandit.

That's the power of print; it even wakes me up at night, nowadays, these years later, with a bad dream of the lonely mountaintops and the hunters closing in on me through the night.

# Acknowledgments

"Speedy's Desert Dance" by Max Brand first appeared in Street & Smith's *Western Story Magazine* (1/28/33). Copyright © 1933 by Street & Smith Publications, Inc. Copyright © renewed 1960 by Dorothy Faust. Copyright © 2008 by Golden West Literary Agency for restored material. Acknowledgment is made to Condé Nast Publications, Inc., for their co-operation.

"A Watch and the Wilderness" by Max Brand appeared in *Elk's Magazine* (9/40). Copyright © 1940 by Elks National Memorial and Publication Commission. Copyright © renewed 1968 by the Estate of Frederick Faust. Copyright © 2008 by Golden West Literary Agency for restored material.

"The Good Badman" by George Owen Baxter first appeared in Street & Smith's *Western Story Magazine* (1/30/26). Copyright © 1926 by Street & Smith Publications, Inc. Copyright © renewed 1953 by Dorothy Faust. Copyright © 2008 by Golden West Literary Agency for restored material. Acknowledgment is made to Condé Nast Publications, Inc., for their co-operation.

# About the Author

Max Brand is the best-known pen name of Frederick Faust, creator of Dr. Kildare, Destry, and many other fictional characters popular with readers and viewers worldwide. Faust wrote for a variety of audiences in many genres. His enormous output, totaling approximately 30,000,000 words or the equivalent of 530 ordinary books, covered nearly every field: crime, fantasy, historical romance, espionage, Westerns, science fiction, adventure, animal stories, love, war, and fashionable society, big business and big medicine. Eighty motion pictures have been based on his work along with many radio and television programs. For good measure he also published four volumes of poetry. Perhaps no other author has reached more people in more different ways.

Born in Seattle in 1892, orphaned early, Faust grew up in the rural San Joaquin Valley of California. At Berkeley he became a student rebel and one-man literary movement, contributing prodigiously to all campus publications. Denied a degree because of unconventional conduct, he embarked on a series of adventures culminating in New York City where, after a period of near starvation, he received simultaneous recognition as a serious poet and successful author of fiction. Later, he traveled widely, making his home in New York, then in Florence, and finally in Los Angeles.

Once the United States entered the Second World War, Faust abandoned his lucrative writing career and his work as a screenwriter to serve as a war correspondent with the infantry in Italy, despite his fifty-one years and a bad heart. He was killed during a night attack on a hilltop village held by the German army. New books based on magazine serials or unpublished manuscripts or restored versions continue to appear so that, alive or dead, he has averaged a new book every four months for seventy-five years. Beyond this, some work by him is newly reprinted every week of every year in one or another format somewhere in the world. A great deal more about this author and his work can be found in *The Max Brand Companion* (Greenwood Press, 1997) edited by Jon Tuska and Vicki Piekarski.